"Why are you here?" he asked softly.

Moisture misted Andrea's eyes. She hoped he didn't see it. He wouldn't, couldn't, understand that seeing him again was peeling her away layer by layer until there was nothing left of her but a beating heart.

She took a step toward him. "I'm here because I need you, Tony."

Tony studied her from beneath his dark lashes. He'd never expected to see Andrea again. Now here she was, saying she needed him. He couldn't imagine why. Andrea Rawlins had never wanted for anything.

It was incredible how beautiful she had grown. Six years ago in El Paso he'd been enchanted by her sultry dark hair, her turquiose-blue eyes and her skin like warm honey. He had thought then that if she'd been any more beautiful it would be too much for a man to bear. That thought was coming home to him now.

Dear Reader:

Happy Holidays! All the best wishes to you for a joyful, loving holiday season with your family and friends.

And while celebrating, I hope that you think of Silhouette Romance. Our authors join me in wishing you a wonderful holiday season, and we have some treats in store for you during November and December—as well as during the exciting new year.

Experience the magic that makes the world so special for two people falling in love. Meet heroines that will make you cheer for their happiness and heroes (be they the boy next door or a handsome, mysterious stranger) that will win your heart. Silhouette Romances reflect the magic of love—sweeping you away with books that will make you laugh and cry, heartwarming, poignant stories that will move you time and time again.

During the next months, we're publishing romances by many of your all-time favorites such as Diana Palmer, Brittany Young, Lucy Gordon and Victoria Glenn. Your response to these authors and others in Silhouette Romances has served as a touchstone for us, and we're pleased to bring you more books with Silhouette's distinctive medley of charm, wit and—above all—*romance*.

I hope you enjoy this book and the many stories to come. Come home to Silhouette Romance—for always!

Sincerely,

Tara Hughes
Senior Editor
Silhouette Books

STELLA BAGWELL

Cactus Rose

Published by Silhouette Books New York

America's Publisher of Contemporary Romance

For my mother, Lucille, to prove
to her that there is romance in the desert.
Thanks, Mama, for going all those miles with us.

SILHOUETTE BOOKS
300 E. 42nd St., New York, N.Y. 10017

ISBN: 0-373-08621-0

First Silhouette Books printing December 1988

Printed in the U.S.A.

Books by Stella Bagwell

Silhouette Romance

Golden Glory #469
Moonlight Bandit #485
A Mist on the Mountain #510
Madeline's Song #543
The Outsider #560
The New Kid in Town #587
Cactus Rose #621

STELLA BAGWELL

is a small-town girl and an incurable romantic—a combination she feels enhances her writing. When she isn't at her typewriter, she enjoys reading, listening to music, sketching pencil drawings and sewing her own clothes. Most of all, she enjoys exploring the outdoors with her husband and young son.

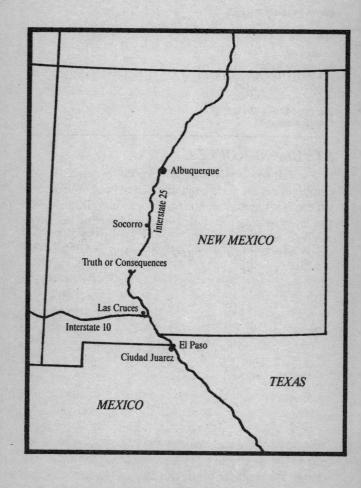

Chapter One

Andrea Rawlins turned the pages of the ledger with a hopeless sigh and leaned back in the rich leather chair.

A brass desk lamp shed a small pool of light on the massive oak desk; otherwise, the room was dark.

Reluctantly her eyes were drawn back to the spot-lighted pages. Like someone unable to tear her gaze from an unfolding tragedy, she continued to scan the facts and figures.

The book summed up everything. There was only one conclusion: if something wasn't done soon, she was going to lose the ranch.

Rio Vista—the river ranch. She leaned forward, resting her forearms against the edge of the desk. Beyond the desk was a row of tall, small-paned windows. Through the glass, the light of the moon tipped the palm trees with a delicate silver glow and shimmered across the water of the oval pool in the courtyard below.

If Andrea looked further, she would see a row of stables filled with the finest quarter horses money could buy, barns big enough to hold two or three houses and, beyond the barns, acres and acres of pastureland dotted with a vast herd of purebred Santa Gertrudis.

But Andrea didn't see any of this. At the moment she was pressing the heels of her palms against her eyes, wondering how she was going to sleep tonight, knowing tomorrow would not bring any hope.

Slowly she rose from the desk, then switched off the lamp. The moonlight was strong enough to illuminate her path out of the study. In the quiet darkness she climbed the curved staircase, then at the landing turned to the right. Her bedroom was only two doors down from her daughter's room.

Her bedroom. She'd slept alone there since she and her husband, Keith, were divorced four years ago. The parting had not devastated her as many would have expected.

Andrea had married Keith believing he was interested only in her. Too late she discovered he'd been more attracted to the wealth that came with the Rawlins name than to her. She'd severed all ties with Keith and resumed her maiden name.

Inside Andrea's bedroom there were sliding glass doors leading out onto a balcony, which ran the length of the house and looked down on the courtyard below.

Here in El Paso, almost everything had a Spanish-Mexican flavor. The ranch house, with its creamy stuccoed walls, red-tiled roof and graceful curving archways, was typical.

Andrea walked over to the wide glass panels and looked out at the night. City lights twinkled beneath the stars and moonlight. To the right, not too far away, was the muddy, sluggish Rio Grande winding its path through the desert hills. Just beyond the river, the lights of Ciudad Juárez blended with those of El Paso.

Thoughts of her father reared up once again, reminding her that his death had brought a myriad of problems to the ranch. Down through the years, Andrea supposed she'd made the mistake of thinking him invincible. Roy Rawlins had been one of those tough men who worked hard, lived hard and played hard. He'd built himself a cattle empire—one of the biggest along the border. The last thing Andrea had expected was for him to die so young and so suddenly, leaving it all to her.

It had been one year since his death, and in that time she'd discovered that her father had mortgaged the ranch heavily. Apparently he'd put the borrowed money into business ventures that had failed to make a profit.

Andrea realized that at this point it didn't make any difference what her father had done with the money. Knowing where it had gone wouldn't alter the fact that bank deadlines must be met or the ranch would no longer be hers.

Struggling to shake these worries, she began to undress in the darkness. Once she'd pulled a white silk robe over her graceful curves, she crossed the room and entered a private bath. There she switched on the light and her image flashed at her from all directions.

Ignoring the mirrored tiles on the wall, she stood in front of the vanity and stared at herself. She was twenty-five, but most of the time she felt much older.

Leaning closer to the mirror, she pushed a silky chocolate-brown lock away from her face and let it fall back with the long tresses that curled loosely against her back. Everyone had always told her what beautiful eyes she had; large, turquoise blue, rimmed with thick sable lashes so long they sometimes looked unreal.

Andrea doubted her eyes were that beautiful now. Beneath them, dark smudges gave her a hollow, exhausted look. The lines between her finely arched brows and the usually smooth skin around her bow-shaped mouth tightened with worry.

Listlessly she smoothed her fingers over the honey-colored skin molding her high cheekbones. The healthy rose blush that usually touched her cheeks wasn't evident tonight. Her skin had a lackluster quality about it and she was disgusted at the image staring back at her.

Yet what did she expect? She'd worked nonstop for the past month, contacting buyers and lenders, juggling money from one account to another in order to meet the mounting debts of the ranch. Then there were the nights, she thought grimly, the nights she had lain awake, worry gripping every thought, tightening every nerve in her body until she lay like a taut guitar string, afraid to close her eyes, afraid to fall asleep and discover what the morning might bring.

She couldn't let it keep happening. She wouldn't allow it! With jerky determined movements she rubbed cleansing cream onto her face, then wiped it clean.

It was already past eleven, and Sara had been in bed for hours. Andrea would stop by her daughter's room then go downstairs and drink a glass of wine before she went to bed. Maybe that would be enough to let her relax and fall asleep.

Andrea found the five-year-old girl curled into a secure little ball, her dark wavy hair fanned against the pillow.

She smiled faintly and reached down to straighten the sheet across the small sleeping child. Even though Andrea tried to make her daughter wear braids to bed to keep the tangles from her hair, Sara wouldn't hear of it. She wanted to be big and wear her hair loose like her mama's.

Andrea looked down at her daughter with a wealth of love. It was unfortunate that Keith had never been close to his daughter while he and Andrea were married. To him, Sara had merely been a kid, a responsibility to be shifted to someone else. He'd always been so absorbed by his own needs, she thought.

Yet it had been an entirely different matter with Roy. His granddaughter had been the light of his life. He'd taken her practically everywhere with him. Especially on the ranch, where he was fond of telling her cowboy stories and how someday she would grow up to inherit the Rio Vista.

Needless to say, Roy's death had been much more traumatic for Sara than her father moving thousands of miles away had been. Keith had proved to be selfish and irresponsible. A man like that could never be an anchor in anyone's life, much less take care of a family. Andrea and Sara had always looked to Roy for that. His passing had left a void in their lives.

The responsibilities Roy had left behind had fallen on Andrea's young shoulders with a great thud. This past year had been very difficult for Andrea both emotionally and financially. Her father had taught her all about cows and horses, but he'd never taught her the business side of running an operation as big as the Rio Vista.

Consequently she was learning as she went along. Her father's debts were handicapping her, but even so, Andrea was determined to hang on to the ranch. Roy had promised his granddaughter that someday it would belong to her. If nothing else, Andrea had to fulfill that promise.

Andrea was pulling Sara's door closed when she caught the sound of a footstep behind her. Turning, she saw Rosita, the housekeeper, ambling toward her.

"*Niña*, it's late. Why aren't you in bed?" she scolded. "How long do you think you can keep up this pace?"

Rosita had lived on the ranch for nearly twenty years. She and her husband, Luis, had raised their six sons on the Rio Vista. Andrea thought, not for the first time, that Rosita seemed more like the mistress of the place than she did.

Andrea's mother, Jenny, had died more than ten years ago of a debilitating kidney disease. After that, Rosita had quickly stepped in and been like a mother to Andrea. She loved the older woman deeply.

"I was just checking on Sara," she told Rosita, her voice husky with unshed tears.

Rosita reached over and clicked on an overhead light. With stern black eyes she studied Andrea's desolate expression.

"You've been fretting and crying," she accused in her heavy accent.

Andrea shook her head. "I haven't been crying."

Rosita's heavy bosom rose on a deep breath. "Then you have been thinking about it!"

If Andrea hadn't been so sick at heart she would have laughed at Rosita's reasoning. "I haven't been thinking about crying," she insisted. "I've been thinking none of us are going to have a roof over our heads if something doesn't change. The death of that last bull has really hurt matters."

Rosita shook her head sadly. "If Roy had been here that would never have happened. I blame that man you have managing things, *niña*. He seems to spend more time in the city than here on the ranch."

"He's still learning, Rosita. If I give him more time he might—"

"Let half the herd die? No, Andrea, something needs to be done now, tomorrow! I know I have told you this before, but if you would go to Antonio, he could help you. He will know what to do."

Andrea frowned doubtfully at the mention of Rosita's son. "Tony hasn't been on this ranch in six years. How could you possibly believe he would want to help me now?"

Rosita's expression softened and she took a step forward and smoothed her wrinkled hand over Andrea's hair. "This place was Tony's home for a long time. And you were his friend. He will help, I promise."

Andrea sighed listlessly. "It would be asking too much of him."

The old woman struck her forehead in frustration. "The time has come for you to ask someone!"

Rosita was right about that much. "Even if he were willing to help," Andrea countered, "Tony has his own ranch to run. He couldn't leave Albuquerque just to come down here and work on the Rio Vista."

"Are you afraid to see Tony?" Rosita asked. "Are you afraid you'll remember the crush you had on him, how sad you were when he went away?"

Andrea's lip quivered, but she tried to deny that Rosita had hit a nerve. "Don't be ridiculous—I'm not afraid to see Tony."

Rosita folded her arms across her breast with a loud snort. "Then there is no problem. I'll have your suitcases packed by the time you finish breakfast in the morning. Then you're going to drive to Alburquerque."

"Rosita—not tomorrow! I have to—"

"You have to do as I tell you! And if Tony turns you down—then he's no son of mine!"

Before Andrea could make another protest, Rosita had whirled around and started down the staircase.

Andrea watched the woman disappear into the darkness. Perhaps Rosita was right. Tony had always loved the Rio Vista and he was very knowledgeable about ranching. He would be a great help if he would agree to make the trip to El Paso.

The exchange with Rosita made Andrea forget the glass of wine. Deep in thought, she walked back to her bedroom and clicked on the light. Across the room was a long oak dresser covered with her personal things.

On one end of the dresser was a carved wooden jewelry box. From one of the little drawers she pulled a silver bracelet with a disk-shaped charm.

It had been a long time since she'd taken out the bracelet. Lifting it up to the light, Andrea fingered the disk and read the inscription, even though she knew exactly what was written. To Andrea, Always, Tony.

Always, Tony.

Funny how those words still had the power to mock her, to stab at that most tender part of her heart. Andrea had taken them so literally at the time, and that had been her mistake. Since then she'd learned *always* didn't mean *forever*.

Keith had come across the bracelet once and asked Andrea who Tony was. She'd answered simply—a friend who had worked for her dad. And that much had been true.

By the time Tony was twenty-eight, he had been foreman on the Rio Vista for five years.

Tony Ramirez had been nine years older than Andrea. Not a great difference, but enough to make him intriguing to a young girl. Since his family had come to the ranch when Tony was young, he'd spent most of his life on the Rio Vista, just like Andrea. They should have been equals, but it had not been the case. She was the owner's daughter whereas he'd merely been the son of the hired help.

To Andrea, the difference had never seemed important. He was simply Tony, the boy she'd secretly had a crush on for as long as she could remember. He was the most handsome, the most charming, the most understanding man to walk the face of the earth.

Since they both shared a great love of cutting horses, the two of them had spent many hours together grooming, riding and training them. She remembered how he'd always teased her, giving her those faint little half smiles of his that made her think there was more going on behind his hazel eyes than what he was telling her. There had always been a quiet, gentle strength about him, too. An assurance that made her feel very safe with him, made her able to talk to him about anything and know that he would understand.

They'd done so many things together, shared so much laughter, she thought with a touch of sadness.

Her lips curled with a bit of mockery. That was in the past, Andrea. Love, friendship, closeness, whatever a person wanted to label it, had a habit of changing between two people. Still, she wished it hadn't changed. She wished she could go to Albuquerque in the morning and find that when she got there, Tony would be the same, that she could rest her head upon his strong chest and pour her heart out to him.

She closed her fist around the bracelet, squeezing the silver until the disk cut painfully into her palm. Then, angry with herself for having let her memories get so out of control, she shoved the bracelet back into the jewelry box and pushed the drawer closed.

Her white silk robe floated through the darkness as she made her way down the stairs and entered the living room. A wet bar was built into one corner next to the arched windows looking out over the courtyard. Without bothering to turn on the light, Andrea crossed to it and poured herself a glass of wine.

She carried it to one of the window seats, where she sipped it slowly and stared across the moon-shadowed courtyard. Leaning her cheek against the arch framing the window, she recalled how the courtyard had looked on the night of her nineteenth birthday.

Roy had gone all out for the occasion and Rosita had prepared a big Texas-style barbecue. The long tables set out near the pool had creaked under the weight of the food. It had been a party that many of her friends still remembered. It was the time Tony had given her the bracelet. How happy she'd been about the gift. But she couldn't forget how sad she had felt when he had spent nearly the entire evening with the other hired hands. He had set himself apart from Andrea and her circle of friends, and she had not wanted it to be that way. To Andrea, Tony Ramirez had always been much more than a hired hand.

The next morning, Andrea was in the midst of eating a warm corn tortilla spread with butter and honey when Rosita said, "Your things are packed, Andrea. Since it's so warm, I put in a skirt instead of jeans."

"Mama, are you going somewhere?" Sara asked.

Frustrated, Andrea arched a brow at Rosita. It was just like the older woman to bring up the trip in front of Sara before Andrea had had the opportunity to speak to her daughter about it.

She knew Rosita's ploy. It would be very difficult to argue about the trip in front of Sara. It was no use telling Rosita she had already decided on her own to go to Albuquerque and see Tony.

"Just for today and tomorrow. I'm going to drive up to Albuquerque, darling. Remember? That's the place where we went to the fair."

Last night Andrea had realized it was time to make a move, to change, to fight the problems facing her. If Tony could help, then she had to at least try talking to him. Seeing him again would be—well, it would be nice. Just thinking about it made her heart pound in anticipation.

"May I go, too? Is it time for the fair again?"

Andrea smiled gently at her daughter. "No. It isn't time yet for the fair. And since I'm going on business, you'll have to stay with Rosita."

Sara pressed her little lips into a sulky pout. "It wouldn't hurt for me to go. Please, Mama. Please—"

Andrea shook her head. She couldn't manage Sara on this trip. Confronting Tony about the ranch would need her undivided attention.

"Be a good girl, Sara. Mama will take you next time—when the fair is going. That isn't too far off. And I'm sure if you're sweet to Rosita, she'll let you help her bake cookies."

The little girl frowned and plunked her chin down on her tiny fist. "I don't want to bake cookies. I want to go with you."

Andrea sighed and looked at Rosita. The housekeeper said, "Maybe Jenny can come over and swim in the pool with you. If you're a good girl, I'll call her mother this morning and see if it's okay with her."

Sara's features brightened at Rosita's suggestion. Jenny was her dearest friend. "Do you think her mother will say yes?" she asked the housekeeper.

"I'm sure she will," Rosita said as she ladled scrambled eggs with green chilies and cheese onto the girl's plate. "Now eat so you can grow up like your mama."

Andrea smiled as Sara obediently dipped into the eggs. "I'll be back home before you even miss me," she assured her.

"Who are you going to see, Mama?"

Andrea reached for her coffee. "A friend."

"What's her name? Do I know her?"

Andrea shook her head. "His name is Tony. And no, you don't know him."

"How do you know him?"

Once again, Andrea looked over to Rosita, who was busily stacking dishes in the dishwasher.

"Tony used to live here on the ranch," Rosita explained patiently. "Tony is my little boy."

Sara smothered a giggle. "Why do you wanta see a little boy, Mama?"

Andrea laughed. "Tony isn't a little boy anymore. He is a grown man. Like your grandpa Roy was."

"Did he know my grandpa Roy?" Sara asked eagerly, always ready to talk about her grandfather. Andrea knew her daughter still missed the paternal affection Roy had given her.

"Yes, he did, sweetheart. They were great friends."

"Like me and Jenny?" Sara asked after gulping down a drink of orange juice.

Andrea nodded. "Tony worked for your grandpa. He helped him take care of the cows and horses."

"Now Tony has a ranch of his own," Rosita proudly told Sara. "After breakfast I'll show you a letter he sent me and a picture of him. If you eat all your eggs," she tacked on in motherly fashion.

Sara clapped her hands together with anticipation and dug into her food.

"If he was friends with grandpa Roy, will you ask him to come visit us?" Sara said between bites of egg.

Andrea smiled, hoping it would be as simple as Sara made it sound. "Yes, I'll ask him. Now eat your breakfast, then you can help me carry my things out to the car."

* * *

The morning was already hot by the time Andrea pulled her little white sports car onto Interstate 10. It was a dry desert heat, it would be in the mid-nineties by afternoon.

Andrea settled herself more comfortably behind the steering wheel, thinking of the small suitcase on the back seat. It was more than two hundred and sixty miles to Albuquerque. After driving that far, she'd hardly feel like turning around and heading back that night. Still, she wished she didn't have to be away from Sara and the ranch overnight.

But perhaps it would be good for both of them, she decided. Especially Sara, who was spoiled by her mother's constant attention. And as for Andrea, she'd been bogged down by the ranch's problems nonstop since Roy's death. It would be good to see Albuquerque again. She only wished she was going for a different reason.

It had been six years since Tony left the Rio Vista, and although his mother and father heard from him regularly, he'd never talked or written to Andrea. She had no idea how he would react to seeing her again. Not knowing gnawed at her nerves.

Since it was Friday, traffic was congested all the way through to Las Cruces, where she veered onto Interstate 25, which ran through the heart of New Mexico.

Texas, Mexico, New Mexico—to her it was all the same, even though she'd been born and raised in El Paso. Her fellow Texans would shame her for that thought, but it was in her heart anyway. To Andrea, it was all the southwest desert, a place she loved.

To many, the bald desert mountains held no beauty, but to Andrea they were magnificent. The vast open-

ness, the choya, the yucca, the sagebrush and creosote and the twisted mesquite trees possessed a beauty
all their own.

The Rio Grande followed the highway to Albuquerque, sometimes to the left of her, sometimes to the
right. Often she could not see the water, but Andrea
knew it was there as she passed the orchards of pecan
trees, the irrigated fields of alfalfa, corn and other
crops.

Towns and settlements followed the river's banks,
sucking at its life-giving moisture in this dry thirsty
land. Away from the river there was nothing but open
space. Andrea drove for long stretches without seeing
towns, people, animals or much vegetation. She supposed it would frighten some people to drive alone
through such isolation. But it did not frighten her.

She had brought a supply of water with her and a
few snacks. The U.S. Border Patrol was always traveling the highway, searching for illegal immigrants
who might have crossed at El Paso. They would give
her help if she needed it.

Andrea stopped once in Socorro for gas and a can
of lemonade. It was only an hour or so to the Rocking R ranch. Rosita had given her directions—through
Albuquerque, then five miles west and south of Interstate 40.

When the beautiful city of Albuquerque loomed on
the horizon, Andrea almost wished she would get lost
so that she could go back home and tell Rosita the
ranch had been impossible to find. But the older
woman would never believe that. Andrea could find a
jackrabbit in a dust storm; she could easily find a
ranch as large as the Rocking R and Rosita knew it.

Andrea was getting an attack of nerves and she couldn't understand why. Tony was an old friend. She could ask anything of him, couldn't she?

Thinking back, Andrea admitted she'd been terribly hurt when he'd suddenly left the ranch. She'd wanted to ask him several things back then, like why he was choosing to make his life away from his family and the Rio Vista, and didn't his close friendship with Andrea count for anything? But Tony had left before she'd had the chance to confront him.

At the moment, Andrea could only think that they had never even said goodbye to each other.

Chapter Two

Rocking R Ranch. Andrea read the words on the wooden sign as she steered her little white car across a cattle guard. The gravel road turned into hard powdered earth.

Dust billowed in the wake of the car as the road curved and wound through the sage and choya. In front of her the rutted track climbed gradually toward the sinking red-orange sun.

This morning, before Andrea left El Paso, Rosita had tried to call Tony. His housekeeper had told her he was out but would be back home later in the day. The woman had assured Rosita she would let Tony know that Andrea was driving up to see him.

Now it was late afternoon; Andrea wondered if Tony would be home. The question brought an unnatural dryness to her throat. She told herself not to be nervous. She was merely meeting a man. *A man who was once an important part of your life,* she tacked on. *But don't think about that now. Think about the present and the reason you've come so far to see him.*

The house was a low rambling L-shape built of rose-beige stucco. Compared to the house Andrea lived in, it was a very modest size. Even so, the home was an indication of a prosperous life-style.

As Andrea drew closer she was impressed with the landscaping. Obviously, someone kept the carpet of green grass inside the rail fence that separated the front yard form the desert pasture meticulously cut and watered. Yucca plants grew close to the house. Their long stalks were heavy with white blossoms. Red geraniums lined the walk and bordered the front portico.

Andrea pulled the car to a halt just outside the front fence. Her legs were cramped from the long drive. She climbed from beneath the steering wheel with slow stiff movements. She was just brushing the wrinkles from her denim skirt when she heard the sound of a door slamming.

Heart pounding, she lifted her head and looked toward the house. It wasn't Tony who stood at the top of the steps but a woman. The housekeeper, Andrea guessed. The woman's petite frame was clothed in faded denims and a plaid Western shirt, the long tails tied in a knot at her waist. A red bandanna covered her short cap of blond hair. Andrea figured she was, at the most, in her late fifties.

"Good afternoon," she said. "I suppose you're Andrea?"

Andrea smiled warmly at the woman. "Yes—I am. And you're Zelda?"

Returning her smile, Zelda moved off the porch. Andrea met her at the gate.

"Rosita called again a few minutes ago," she said. "She wanted to make sure you'd arrived safely."

Andrea nodded. "She worries about me," she explained.

"I'll call her back and let her know you're here."

"That's very kind of you."

Zelda opened the gate and motioned for Andrea to pass through. "Tony's mother is a protective soul. And she obviously considers you one of her own." She looked over at Andrea. "You've come a long way. You must be exhausted from the drive. Did you make the trip okay?"

"No trouble at all." Andrea glanced rather sheepishly at the woman as they walked up the sidewalk. "I—I hope I haven't come at a bad time. Actually it was—"

Zelda shook her head. "Anytime is the right time. Tony's mother told me why you're here. You don't need to explain things."

Andrea felt herself blushing. Just what had Rosita told the woman? When she got back to El Paso she was certainly going to find out!

Before Andrea could reply, Zelda glanced at her. Her expression was apologetic. "Sorry, Andrea. My hubby says I'm always doing that. Saying things that don't come out just right. What I was trying to say is that you're welcome here at the Rocking R anytime. No need for invitation or explanation."

Andrea smiled gratefully at the woman. Apparently Zelda had worked for Tony for a long time. She obviously felt the ranch was home to her, too. She was making this whole situation much easier for Andrea. "Thank you, Zelda. Was Tony surprised to hear I was coming?" She couldn't keep herself from asking.

Zelda's thinly arched brows pulled together in a faint frown. "Tony hasn't been back to the ranch house, so he doesn't know yet. But that's hardly a problem. He's going to be happy to see a pretty thing like you—and especially an old friend."

An old friend. Is that what she was to Tony? She felt like so much more but wondered how he felt.

By now they had reached the house. Zelda pushed the door open and allowed Andrea to precede her into the room's cool interior.

The first thing Andrea noticed was that the windows and doors did not shut in an air-conditioned climate. Yet the house was pleasantly cool and breezy from the overhead ceiling fans. It was a house built to hold out the desert heat with its cool tiled floors, spacious uncluttered rooms, shaded windows and white walls. The furniture was all varnished pine with very simple lines. The colors ranged from sage blue to earth brown with touches of orange and yellow here and there. It was all very nice, very spotless. Andrea loved it at first glance.

Zelda led her into a den and told her to make herself comfortable while she went for refreshments. Andrea wanted to ask her when she thought Tony would come home, but the woman left the room before she had the chance. She wished Zelda had told him she was coming. But it could hardly be helped now.

Moments later, Zelda reappeared with a tray laden with a jug of tea, a pot of sugar, a saucer of lemon and lime wedges and a tall glass filled with crushed ice. Beside all this, there was a selection of cookies and fruit.

Andrea looked guiltily at the woman. "This is very kind of you. I'm causing you all kinds of extra work."

Zelda waved away Andrea's words. "No trouble. Just kick back and relax while I go start dinner. Tony should be back within an hour. You will stay the night, won't you? There's hardly any need to drive back to Albuquerque when Tony has lots of room. I'll fix up one of the bedrooms before I leave."

Andrea's eyes widened as the woman spoke. So Zelda wasn't a live-in housekeeper. And she expected Andrea to stay here tonight? Well, why not? Tony wasn't a stranger, and she hated to think of driving all the way to Albuquerque to find a motel room.

"If you think Tony won't mind," she said as Zelda turned to go.

The woman's questioning glance asked Andrea why Tony should mind.

"Tony might be going out or having friends over. I'd be an unexpected burden," Andrea reasoned.

Zelda chuckled with obvious amusement. "Tony rarely goes out or has friends over. He's a homebody."

A homebody? Tony Ramirez, the guy who'd loved to go dancing every chance he got? Andrea opened her mouth to disagree, but by then Zelda had disappeared and a sudden clatter of pans could be heard down the breezeway.

Andrea poured herself a glass of tea and carried it to a seat that overlooked the front yard. Beyond the fence and her car was a broad range of low rolling hills. In the far distance, a herd of Herefords grazed at the tough scraggly grass growing between the sage, cactus and creosote. On the eastern horizon, just edging the city of Albuquerque, was the Sangre de Cristo mountain range. It was a beautiful view. Andrea wished that she could see it in the wintertime when the mountains were capped with snow.

She supposed the herd of cattle belonged to Tony. For as far as she could see, there weren't any other houses or ranches around.

About thirty minutes later, a motor hummed outside, but Andrea didn't hear it. She was just hanging up the telephone after talking to her daughter and reassuring Rosita she had made the trip safely. She didn't expect to see Tony as she sat down and stared out the window at the lengthening shadows.

A footstep alerted her, but by then it was too late to prepare herself for the sight of him. Andrea stiffened, wondering why her heart was pounding out of control.

"Andrea."

"Hello, Tony," she said softly.

His deep voice was still a wonderful sound. It released the tension from her stiff body. Sliding from the seat, Andrea stood and met his gaze.

Before her was the same Tony she had known, and yet he wasn't that same man at all. Six years had made a great difference in his appearance. His face had become lean with hollows in his cheeks. The cleft in his chin seemed much deeper and the shadow of whiskers along his jaw much thicker. The dark brown hair he'd worn long was now trimmed stylishly close to his head. But it was not these things she noticed the most. It was his eyes. The beautiful hazel eyes that had always been filled with mischief and laughter were now sharp and narrowed.

"Hello," he said, moving further into the room.

"Did Zelda tell you I was here?" she asked him.

He nodded, then quickly asked, "Has something happened to Mama or Papa?"

Andrea hadn't stopped to think he might connect her presence with his parents. She hated to think he might have been unduly alarmed. "No," she assured him hastily. "They're—they're just fine. As fit as ever."

A look of relief crossed Tony's face. He reached up and pulled the black broad-brimmed hat from his head. Glancing away from her, he ran his hands through his hair, then turned back. His eyes were still narrowed, and she stood immobile beneath their sharp gaze.

Time. Why did it have to move on? Why did it have to change things and people? Why couldn't she turn back the years? Bring back the Tony she used to know? Right now she yearned to see the young Tony, not this cold man before her.

But then, she'd changed, too, Andrea realized. She no longer looked nineteen. Her body had ripened and matured after she'd had Sara. Her face had acquired a womanly look; she was no longer a tender innocent woman-child.

She'd worn a straight skirt of heavy faded denim and a loose white shirt cinched at the waist with a belt of silver conchas. Western boots of soft fawn-colored leather covered her feet and most of her calves. Her dark hair was loose and curled against her back, her lips still stained with cherry-colored lipstick. She wondered if Tony thought she had changed as much as she thought he had.

"I—I never expected to see you here," he finally said.

She smiled. "Rosita called this morning, but Zelda said you'd already gone out. I hope I didn't give you too much of a scare."

He walked across the room and tossed his hat onto the desk in the corner of the room. "Mama and Papa are getting older. You never know when something could happen."

"Something can happen at any age," she said.

He looked back at her, a rueful expression creasing his dark features. "I guess you should know. I was sorry to hear about your father."

Tony had sent flowers to Roy's funeral, but he hadn't come. Still, Andrea knew the loss was bound to have cut into him deeply.

"Thank you, Tony," she responded quietly.

Tony's lips quirked with faint regret and suddenly he found he could not look at her any longer. He turned his back to her and took a deep painful breath.

"Mama tells me you have a daughter. How is she?"

Andrea placed her glass of tea back onto the tray. She glanced at the taut line of Tony's broad shoulders and something tightened in her throat. "Growing like a weed," she said, trying to force a cheerful note to her voice. "She's almost six. She'll start school this fall."

Through his parents, Tony knew Andrea had been divorced from her husband for a couple of years now. He also knew that her former husband had turned out to be a sorry character. Yet he expected losing Roy had been far harder on Andrea than her failed marriage. It hurt Tony to think of her going through such tragedy, but he couldn't say any of these things to her. She was no longer the teenage girl he used to know.

Jamming his hands into the front pockets of his jeans, he turned around to face her.

Andrea wondered why the room seemed so quiet, why it seemed so hot and stifling when earlier it had been very pleasant.

"And how is El Paso?" he asked with a shrug of one shoulder.

"Hot."

His eyes settled on her mouth. "It's supposed to be hot."

She'd been standing in the same spot since he'd walked into the room, but she didn't realize it. She swallowed and met his gaze. "Tony—I—"

"Why are you here?" he asked softly.

Moisture misted her eyes. She hoped he couldn't see it. He wouldn't, couldn't, understand that seeing him again was peeling her away layer by layer until there was nothing left of her but a beating heart.

She took a step toward him. "I'm here because I need you, Tony."

Tony's features gave no hint of emotion.

Andrea swallowed in an effort to loosen the suffocating knot in her throat. What was he thinking? she wondered. Why had she blurted out her request like that?

Tony studied her beneath his dark lashes. He'd never expected to see Andrea again. Now here she was, saying she needed him. He couldn't imagine why. Andrea Rawlins had never wanted for anything.

It was incredible how beautiful she had grown. Six years ago in El Paso he'd been enchanted by her sultry dark hair, her turquoise-blue eyes and her skin like warm honey. He had thought then that if she'd been any more beautiful it would be too much for a man to bear. That thought was coming home to him now.

Andrea watched him closely, wondering at the faint grin that was beginning to shape his mouth. Was it teasing or mocking?

"Does El Paso have a shortage of men now?" he asked. "Or just a shortage of men like me?"

Men like him? There were very few men like him, she realized. "All the good-looking ones have left, Tony. So I felt it was my duty to recruit you."

His grin became full grown. "I see you haven't lost your sense of humor."

Andrea smiled faintly. "I've lost a lot of things but hopefully not that."

Tony crossed to the windows and turned his back to her as he stared out across the mesa. Andrea watched as his left hand lifted and curved against the arch of the window frame. His fingers were still long and slim, as was his body. He'd always been whipcord lean, sinewy and strong. A denim shirt, faded from many washings, stretched across the width of his shoulders. A pair of Levi's molded his long legs. His black-booted feet were planted apart. He was just as masculine and sexy as she remembered him.

"Does the Rio Vista look the same?"

His voice was unusually hoarse. For one wild second Andrea wondered if he was close to tears. But that was ridiculous. She couldn't imagine this hard man crying. Maybe the Tony of the past, but not this man.

Andrea pushed her fingers through her hair and walked toward him. "Mostly the same," she answered. "Before he died, Dad added more stables. The house looks just like it always has. We're raising Santa Gertrudis now—but I guess your parents told you that."

She stopped a foot or so away from him and took a deep breath to start over. "I—I've missed you, Tony. The ranch never seemed the same after you left."

His head turned and he looked down at her. The right corner of his mouth lifted, making his lips a mocking slash in his face. "For a long time it didn't seem right being away from it," he confessed.

"That's not surprising. After all, it was your home for many years," she told him.

His eyes deserted hers. "Yes, it was. But now the Rocking R is my home."

Andrea did her best to smile, but it was very hard when all she could think of was how much his leaving had hurt. "Now you're more than a foreman. You must be very happy about that."

Andrea was glad for him. She truly was, because she had always wanted the very best for Tony.

A muscle quirked faintly in his dark cheek. "Yeah, I guess I am."

Tony's eyes were hooded, almost brooding. Wasn't he happy with his life? The question raced through Andrea's mind, yet she dared not try to answer it. It would be impossible to know what Tony had been feeling for the past six years.

"Tony—I—" She stepped closer to him and placed her hand on his forearm. Even though it was covered with denim, she could feel it was hard and warm beneath her fingers.

He suddenly turned to her, a faint question in his eyes as they drifted down to where she touched him. "Andrea—why—?"

Footsteps suddenly sounded in the room. Andrea turned to see Zelda standing just inside the arched doorway. She wished the woman hadn't shown up just then.

From the expression on Zelda's face, she knew her timing hadn't been quite right. The sight of Andrea's small hand on Tony's arm and the strained expression on his face were self-explanatory.

"I just wanted to let you know that dinner is ready," she told the two of them. "Everything is on the table."

Tony nodded. "Thanks, Zelda. We'll be right in."

Zelda turned to go. "I'll see you later, then. By the way, Andrea, I made up the room across from Tony's for you and put your case on the nightstand."

Tony turned to Andrea and she wondered why his gaze on her face was more like a touch than a look.

"You're staying here tonight?"

"If—if you don't mind," she answered.

"You honestly didn't think I would, did you?" he asked with surprise.

Andrea shrugged. "It's been a long time, Tony," she answered in an effort to explain her uncertainty.

Tony shook his head. "Not that long," he said, then looked at both women with a faint grin. "Besides, can you imagine what Mama would say if I let you drive back to Albuquerque to get a room?"

Zelda chuckled knowingly. "We'd probably hear Rosita yelling all the way from El Paso."

"Rosita can get loud," Andrea agreed, joining Zelda's chuckles. "Tony can attest to that. She had a time of it trying to break him from walking on her kitchen floor with muddy boots. You could hear her yelling at him all over the house."

Zelda looked at Tony with mischief in her eyes. "It looks like Andrea knows you pretty well. I'll bet she could tell lots of stories about you, Tony," she teased.

Tony smiled and said, "Yes, Andrea knew me better than she should have."

Andrea noticed the smile did not reach his eyes. It made her wonder if his words had a double edge. She kept getting the impression that whatever he'd felt about her and his old life on the Rio Vista, he wanted to put it all behind him.

Zelda didn't seem to find anything amiss. "See you both in the morning," she said with a cherry wave. "Enjoy your dinner. And it was nice meeting you, Andrea. I hope we get to visit before you leave."

Andrea nodded, deciding she liked Tony's housekeeper very much. "Yes, I hope so, too, Zelda. Good night."

The room was unbearably quiet after the woman left. Andrea could hear a vehicle being started out in the back, then the sound of it pulling away. It gave her a strange feeling to know she was alone with Tony.

Nervously she looked at him and was once again struck by his presence. Her blue eyes slid slowly over the strong angles of his face, the wide forehead, prominent cheekbones and dark eyes. If Andrea had not known he was thirty-four, it would have been difficult for her to guess his age. He was at that point in his life where he was prime in looks and stamina, at the age where young women looked at him with adoration and older ones with longing.

Determinedly she pushed the thoughts aside, regretting that the moment she had touched him had passed. Andrea wondered what he had been going to ask her. She would probably never know.

"Come on and I'll show you where to wash," he said, snapping Andrea out of her thoughts.

She nodded and followed him down the wide breezeway. At the end of it he turned to the left and walked down a smaller hallway.

"This will be your room," he told her, stopping at an open doorway near the end of the hall. "There's a private bath. I'm certain Zelda made sure you'll find everything you need. When you're finished, I'll be in the kitchen."

He turned to leave and Andrea stepped into the cool dark bedroom. Suddenly she turned back to him. "Where is the kitchen?"

"Go back to the breezeway. It will be on your right," he said, then disappeared out the door.

Andrea found the bathroom and, after clicking on the light, looked curiously around her. The walls were white here, too, except for the black tile surrounding the tub and shower. Pine enclosed the lavatory. The boards slanted at an angle to give the knots and grains a unique look. A dressing bench to match was built at the end of the tub.

Tony's house was such a contrast to the shabby house he'd grown up in on the Rio Vista. She wondered if he thought much about the difference, or had he taken his steps up the ladder in stride?

After washing her hands with rose-scented soap then drying them on a thick white towel, she looked at the image staring back at her. She didn't look as disheveled as she'd thought. Yet she could see the faint lines of fatigue beneath her eyes.

Quickly she pushed her hair away from her face and left the bathroom. Tony would be waiting for her.

Somehow, someway, she had to let him know her reason for coming.

The kitchen was warmer than the rest of the house, not unpleasantly, though. Andrea realized she was very hungry as she entered the room and breathed in the smell of cooked beef and green chilies. Tony was standing beside the cabinets, gazing out the window. At the sound of her footsteps he turned toward her.

"I hope you don't mind eating in the kitchen. Zelda doesn't use the dining room table unless there's a group coming.

"I don't mind at all," she said honestly. "Right now I'm so hungry I think I could eat standing on my head."

His mouth formed a smile as he pulled out a chair for her. "I remember how well you liked to eat," he said.

She smiled as he took a seat at the end of the table, just to her left. "I still like to eat that way," she confessed. "Only I can't get away with it anymore."

One of his dark brows lifted and she laughed lightly. "I tend to get pudgy," she explained.

His eyes drifted down over the swell of her breasts as if he couldn't believe she ever had to worry about her figure. Andrea felt a heat spread beneath her cheeks.

"Looks like Zelda's fixed pepper steak," he told her.

"Mmm, it smells delicious," Andrea commented. "Can she cook as well as your mama?"

"No one can cook like Mama. You know that."

Andrea laughed softly as he handed her the platter of steak. "Yes, I guess I do know that. Rosita is priceless."

She served herself a portion of the beef, then handed the platter back to him.

"I'm glad to hear they're doing okay," he said. "It's been a while since I last talked with them."

"They send their love," she told him.

He glanced over at her and for a moment his features softened and the light she remembered so well crept into his eyes. Yet it was only there for a flickering moment, then it was gone.

"You have a beautiful place here, Tony. You must be very proud of it."

He shrugged. "It keeps the rain off my head."

She laughed at him and he lifted his eyes to the sight of her white teeth between her cherry-red lips.

"You are being modest now, Tony. And I can't ever remember you being modest."

He grinned, making Andrea's heart warm and glad. "You always said I was conceited."

"You were," she exclaimed with a husky laugh. "You thought you could outride any cowboy from Juárez to Durango. And damned if you couldn't."

"Damned if I couldn't," he repeated softly as he handed her a bowl of stewed vegetables. "Do you still work with quarter horses?"

She nodded and sliced into her steak. "At times. Although I've been too busy lately with Sara, my daughter—and seeing after the ranch."

He looked at her curiously. "So you're not raising and training them to sell now?"

The beef melted in her mouth. She chewed it with pleasure. "No. I wish it were possible. But Sara is still small enough to need lots of attention. And there's always so much work to be done around the ranch.

I'm hoping once Sara is in school all day I'll be able to work with two or three horses.''

''You were always good with horses,'' he said, then spoiled the compliment by adding, ''for a woman.''

Andrea laughed. She knew he was teasing her. ''I never could outride you, Tony, but I could outride all the rest.''

There was a bowl of fried sweet corn thickened with white sauce and jalapeño peppers. Andrea put a healthy portion of it onto her plate, then noticed Tony was watching her movements. She smiled at him self-consciously.

''I didn't stop for lunch,'' she explained.

He shook his head at her words. He hadn't noticed the extra helping she had taken. Actually, he had been thinking back to a time when Roy had invited him to the big house for supper. Her father had wanted to discuss the type of bull he planned to buy for the ranch, but all Tony had remembered about the evening was the way Andrea had looked in the candlelight.

He had recognized then that Andrea could pose trouble for him. With just a little nudge he could fall for her. But Tony had not allowed it. A relationship with the boss's daughter would have spelled disaster.

''There is plenty. Take all you want.''

Andrea noticed that the hooded expression had returned to his face. She wondered what had brought it back. Taking a few more bites of her food, she decided she might as well bring up the subject of the ranch.

''I know you're wondering why I'm here.'' She took a deep breath and looked at him. He was studying her intently and she moistened her lips nervously.

One of his shoulders lifted, then fell with equal grace. "The only thing I can think of is that my parents wanted you to check on me."

She smiled faintly, but inside her heart was jumping with strange little flutters that made her feel giddy. "Your mother did want me to come, but not for that reason." She put her fork down and propped her elbows on the edge of the table and her chin on her folded hands. "I came because of the ranch, Tony. I— I'm afraid I'm going to lose it."

He grimaced in disbelief. "I can't believe that, Andrea."

"It's true," she said quietly, then reached to take up her fork once again. "The ranch is heavily in debt."

He swallowed a piece of the steak, then reached for his glass. "Why?"

"Investments my father made before he died. I didn't know about them until I took over the bookkeeping after he passed away."

Andrea's words shocked him. Roy Rawlins had always been a sound businessman. "What kind of investments?"

Andrea sighed and her eyes dropped to her plate. "Business ventures outside of the ranch."

His fork stopped midway to his mouth as his eyes narrowed on her lowered face. "I take it none of them panned out?"

Andrea lifted her gaze back up to him. The wretched expression on her face spoke volumes. "No. The money is gone and now the loan payments are due."

The look on his face said just how incredible he considered her story. "I can't imagine Roy going out on a limb, especially if he'd been ill."

Andrea shook her head. "He hadn't been ill. The stroke was completely unexpected." Feeling suddenly smothered, she reached for her water glass. After a couple of swallows she said, "I knew that Dad liked to dabble in stocks from time to time. I just never realized he'd gotten into it so deeply. I guess this had happened before, but he'd managed to turn things around. He was probably thinking he could this time, but the stroke took him before he had the chance."

Stunned, Tony leaned back in his chair and slipped his fingers through his dark hair. "Do Mama and Papa know about this?"

Andrea nodded grimly. "They know the ranch is in trouble. They don't exactly know why. They believe it's just due to mismanagement."

His eyes were suspicious. "Why should they think that?"

Andrea met his gaze, knowing she would have to tell him everything if she ever expected him to help her. "We lost a bull last week. Your parents think it's the foreman's fault."

His expression remained unmoved. "And what do you think?"

She shrugged. "It would be hard to say whose fault it was. The vet said the bull had some kind of virus. It wasn't caught in time."

He didn't say anything for a moment. She wondered if he was thinking that she wasn't making sure the men did their jobs. It wasn't the impression she wanted him to have of her. She loved the Rio Vista. Since her father had died, she'd worked hard to keep it going. It was important to Andrea that Tony know this.

"It's hard to tell about those kinds of things," he said finally. "But someone should have noticed he was off his feed."

"That's where your parents think the foreman was negligent. That he wasn't watching the cattle closely enough or having the men doing it."

"And what do you think, Andrea?"

She leaned back in her chair, looking at him as she contemplated his question. "I think I need a better foreman, but at the moment, this one's all I've got."

"Sounds like you should be looking for another one," he observed quietly.

Andrea swallowed nervously and absently fiddled with her water glass. "That's why I came to see you."

His hazel eyes shifted suspiciously over her face. Her complexion seemed a bit paler than it had a few moments earlier. He knew what it was costing her to come here, to admit to her father's failures. On the other hand, it was costing him to hear about them.

The Rio Vista had once been Tony's home. It was still his parents' home. And Andrea—she had been special to him. Right now that was the thing that worried him the most.

Chapter Three

I don't really see how I could help.''

His voice was raspy. The sound of it caused her to shiver inside. ''No one knows ranching better than you, Tony. Right now that's what the Rio Vista needs.''

''Andrea—''

It was obvious that Tony knew what she was going to ask of him. It was also obvious that he was having doubts about it. She didn't understand why. She only knew she had to make him see how badly she needed him. Reaching out with her left hand, Andrea softly closed her fingers around his wrist.

''Don't say no, Tony,'' she pleaded. ''Not yet. I know that you have your own place to see after. And—and I'm not going to ask that much of you. Just a week. One week.''

His gaze fell from hers, his face becoming an impassive mask. "Your main problem is financial. I'm a cowboy, not a C.P.A."

Andrea breathed in deeply, trying her best to hold her composure. This past week she'd reached the point of desperation. Tony was her last chance.

Her fingers unconsciously tightened around his wrist. She needed him to be the old Tony, the Tony who understood everything and always had a way of making her feel better. "I've already been in contact with a C.P.A. He advised me to sell whatever I could in order to pay the loans or at least refinance them. I'll have to sell some of the cattle and horses. That's where you come in," she told him.

"I'm in the business of raising them, not selling them," he said without bothering to look at her.

Flippancy from Tony was hard for Andrea to take. She always remembered him as teasing, kind, understanding. He wasn't showing any of those qualities, and she didn't know why. Perhaps he'd just grown out of them. It was a sad thought.

"Come on, Tony," she said, her voice edged with annoyance. "Every rancher is in the business to sell. Knowing which cattle to sell and when to sell them is a big part of it."

"You've got men working for you. Your foreman should know which cattle should go."

Andrea shook her head. "I don't believe he's had that much experience. He's only worked on the ranch a little less than a year."

He looked up at her silently.

"Tony, this is my home, my livelihood that's at stake," she said desperately. "I want someone I can trust. That's why I came to you—"

Tony pulled his wrist away from her fingers. "I haven't been on the Rio Vista in six years. I don't want to go back."

Tony had never been one to hide his feelings. But from the guarded look on his face, Andrea could safely say he'd changed. Something was definitely hidden behind his cool handsome face.

"Why?"

His eyes flickered. "The Rio Vista is none of my business."

"I'd like to make it your business," she told him.

"You don't know what you're saying or asking of me," he said tightly.

She clenched her hands together in an effort to keep from reaching out to him again. "I'm asking for one week, that's all."

"No, you're asking for much more!" The words exploded from him and Andrea shrank back against her chair.

His outburst stunned her and she frantically searched her mind as to why he should react so negatively to her plea for help. It was true that he hadn't been back to the Rio Vista. Andrea had questioned Rosita many times about this, but she always answered with a vague "he's too busy with the ranch" or "there's no one to take care of things so he can get away."

If that was true, why did his mother expect him to drop everything and come now? No, Andrea thought, there was some other reason Tony didn't want to go back to El Paso.

With a tired grimace, Tony pushed his plate of uneaten food away. "Look, Andrea, I think the best thing for you to do is go home in the morning and find someone else—a cattle buyer—"

"A cattle buyer!" she gasped. "Tony, you know what a cattle buyer would do to me! Take the cream of the crop for the least he could. Where would that leave me? I'd have to try to rebuild the herd with a few culls."

His face was hard, but his voice was soft as he said, "I'm sorry your father did this to you."

Andrea had never had to fight so hard to keep tears at bay. Many people had offered her sympathy since Roy had died, but none of their words had touched her as Tony's did now. It reminded her just how close she had felt to him all those years ago.

She took a deep breath, knowing it would never do for her to cry in front of him. It would only embarrass them both.

Rosita was going to be so disheartened if Tony refused to help. But not nearly as much as Andrea was at this moment. It was obvious that the close friendship they'd once shared had faded for him long ago.

"I—I'm sorry, too, Tony," she said in a quiet voice. "And it was wrong of me to ask so much of you. I guess—well, I've just been feeling a little desperate these past few days." She lifted her head to look at him. It was difficult to tell what he was thinking. His expression was stoic, as if he'd blocked out all sights and sounds around him.

Still, Andrea went on, feeling the need to talk. If she didn't keep talking she would think and feel and hurt. "It was selfish of me to put you on the spot like this. Please forget I ever asked."

He didn't answer and sat there motionless, his dark hair falling over his forehead, his eyes somewhere far away.

Andrea wondered where. Back to when they'd once laughed and talked and shared that rare kind of togetherness that made time with him so special?

Andrea couldn't bear to think of it. She scraped back her chair and hurriedly jumped to her feet.

"I wonder if Zelda left us some coffee. I haven't had any since early this morning." Propelling her thoughts to calmer waters, she looked down the long clean cabinet counters. She spotted a coffee maker at one end. The glass pot was full of freshly brewed coffee. Just to the right of it was a German chocolate cake.

Andrea busied herself cutting two slices, finding cups and saucers and pouring the coffee. Tony's indifference had wounded her. Tomorrow, she promised herself, she would let herself cry as she drove through the desert on her way home. But for now she would pretend that everything was all right. That Tony hadn't really turned away from her plea for help and that the problems on the ranch were not all that insurmountable.

Back at the table, she placed Tony's serving in front of him without asking him if he wanted it. The action caused him to turn his head and look at her, then down at the cake. In silent concession, he reached for his fork.

Andrea took her seat once again and began to eat her cake. It was delicious, and the slow steady action of chewing and swallowing calmed her somewhat.

She thought of Rosita and Sara. They had probably already made the cookies and Sara would have eaten at least half a dozen, ruining her supper. The thought brought a faint curve to her lips.

"My daughter wanted to make the trip with me today. She associates Albuquerque with the state fair. I had to explain to her that it wasn't held at this time of the summer. We drove up and went to the fair last year. Do you ever go to the exhibits?"

"Sometimes. The livestock."

Andrea nodded, determined to move on to less painful topics of conversation. "We looked at many of the horses. They were all beautiful. I had a terrible time with Sara. She wanted to pet every one of them."

"She likes horses?"

"She's a lot like me," she explained. "I sold her small pony this spring and she wasn't too happy about that. Sara's not quite sure she's ready for a big, tall horse yet."

"I suppose my mother dotes on her."

Andrea shrugged. "She doesn't actually dote on her. In fact, Rosita's much more strict than I am. Sara certainly obeys her better than she does me, but then your mother just has a way about her. I guess you haven't forgotten."

He shook his head as if to tell her he hadn't forgotten anything about his parents, his family and his life on the Rio Vista.

"Have you had much rain up here? The desert looks much greener than usual. It's not nearly this green at home."

Tony glanced at her. She was hiding behind the pleasantly spoken words. Even though he had not seen her in all this time, he still knew her. And he knew his refusal to help had shaken her, maybe even hurt her.

He didn't want to hurt Andrea. She didn't deserve that.

"We've had a few afternoon showers. We get much more of them than you do at El Paso."

She had finished her cake and sat sipping her coffee. Tony ate the last bite of his, then rose to his feet.

"I've got to go out and patch a piece of fence. There's a TV in the den or a few paperbacks if you'd like to read."

Andrea glanced up at him. "Oh, would you mind if I came along? I'd love to see a bit more of your ranch."

It wasn't what he wanted. He wanted to get away from her, forget entirely that she was here, but he couldn't bear to see her disappointment again.

"It's still hot outside," he reasoned.

She jumped to her feet and began to roll the sleeves of her shirt up higher onto her elbows. "Since when did I ever notice a little heat?" she asked happily, then glanced back at the table of dirty dishes. "What about those?"

"I'll stack them later. Zelda will do them in the morning."

He walked out of the room and Andrea followed him. Outside, the sun had already sunk in the west. Shadows crept across the desert and painted the sky a rich magenta.

Andrea breathed with deep appreciation as she climbed into an open-top Jeep and waited for Tony to slide behind the steering wheel.

They were in back of the house now. Andrea could see the barns and corrals a couple of hundred feet away. To the south on a short rise was a herd of horses, some dark, some painted. Andrea studied them with interest as Tony drove the Jeep down to the barn.

Once he'd gotten a hammer and steeples, he turned the Jeep around and drove back toward the main road that ran in front of the house. Tony turned south on it so that they passed even closer to the horses.

"That's a beautiful herd of horses," Andrea remarked. "They look like Indian ponies."

"They're mustangs. I heard they were going to be destroyed so I offered to take them."

That was just like him, she thought. "Are any of them broken to ride?"

"Three. Zelda's husband has been helping me with them."

She turned to him and smiled knowingly. "Have you landed on your butt yet?"

His grin was faint but there just the same. "No. Just on my head."

"The safest place for you to land, Antonio Ramirez," she lightly teased and was pleased to see the grin on his face deepen.

The cooling wind from the movement of the Jeep whipped Andrea's hair away from her face. Tony had covered his head with his black hat. She studied him in the growing dusk and realized that no matter the outcome of this trip, she was glad that she had come. She realized that she had wanted to see Tony for so long. Even before Roy had died, she had yearned to see Tony's face, to see him smile at her in a way that only he could do.

She hadn't lied when she told him she'd missed him. She supposed she had missed him every day of her life since he'd gone away.

Her eyes softened on the hard masculine angles of his face. He was good to look at and good to be with, in spite of his harsh attitude. Her eyes slipped a bit lower to where his shirt snaps were loose against his bronze chest. In the left pocket a crumpled pack of cigarettes edged up over the faded denim. Yet Andrea was not thinking about the cigarettes. She was wondering what lay beneath them, what was in his heart as they rode together through the desert twilight. Would tonight be long enough for her to find out?

Not more than a half mile from the house, Tony slowed the Jeep, then parked it on a wide shoulder off the right side of the road.

Andrea climbed down from the seat while Tony gathered the hammer, wire cutters and steeples.

When he started up a washed-out ravine, Andrea swung easily in beside him saying, "Here, let me carry the steeples."

"You should stay by the Jeep, Andrea."

"But I can help," she insisted, then undaunted, smiled at his scowling features. "You know I can."

His green-brown eyes lingered on her face then slid slowly, reluctantly, down to the thrust of her breasts beneath the white blouse, the small inward curve of her waist, then even lower to where the front of her skirt parted, showing her shapely legs as she walked. Andrea spelled trouble. He knew that more than anything.

"It's hot and I don't have to tell you that sidewinders could be out here," he said.

"It's not that hot and I can see where I'm walking. Anyway, I've got on my boots and I'm right here beside you," she reasoned.

She didn't have to remind Tony of her closeness. With each passing second, each step they took, he was aware of her scent, her warmth, her softness. Damn it all, why had she wanted to come out here with him? he thought angrily.

Tony paced his strides a bit more slowly so that she could keep up with him. It took them a few minutes to reach the shelf along which the sagging fence ran. The loose rocks and loamy soil made it difficult to climb.

Once Tony was at the top, he took Andrea's hand in his and pulled her up beside him. Her skin was as soft as he remembered and her fingers clung trustingly to his.

As soon as she had her balance, he let them go abruptly. He figured that, for him, touching Andrea was like an alcoholic tasting whiskey, so forbidden yet so desirable.

Telling himself he had to move away from her, Tony began to inspect the fence. Behind him, Andrea looked out across the desert range. The sun was about to set. Soon it would be dark.

"It really needs new wire," he said. "But I'm going to restretch this for the time being."

Andrea crossed the few steps to him. He was already pulling steeples from the fence post. A soft warm breeze was blowing from the southwest. Andrea turned to it, letting it wash over her face and hair. It was so wonderful to be outdoors instead of looking at bills and accounts, facts and figures that refused to cooperate, and talking on the telephone to people who didn't really care that the ranch was in trouble.

Looking back at Tony, she saw that he was already stretching one of the strings of barbed wire. She quickly reached in the paper sack and pulled out a steeple. "Why don't you let me hammer in the steeple while you keep the wire stretched?" she suggested.

"I can do it. Just hand me the steeple."

"You'd need three hands. Give me the hammer." Andrea snatched the claw hammer from his pocket and began to nail the steeple over the wire and into the post. Once she had driven it as far as the wood would allow, she straightened and smiled up at him. "Now see? That wasn't so hard, was it?"

Andrea had never been afraid of work, Tony realized. His mouth curled into a slow smile as he looked down at her. "You haven't changed, Andrea."

"No, I don't suppose I have," she said, inwardly elated to see the smile on his face.

They worked for several more minutes. Tony stretched the wire taut while Andrea hammered in the steeples.

"Does anyone help you with the ranch work?" she asked him between the blows as she hammered at the fence post.

"Only when extra things need doing. Otherwise, I do it all myself. That way I know it's been done right."

"I'm impressed with this place," she said. "You're making it into a good ranch. But then I knew it would be a good one before I ever saw it. Everyone back home knows you were the best foreman Dad ever had."

Beneath his dark lashes, he watched her work diligently with the hammer. "You must be trying to flatter me."

She glanced up at him and frowned. "Since when did you ever need flattery, Tony? Besides, Dad changed foremen about five or six times after you left. I think that says it all."

Tony wondered if she had become friends with any of those other foremen. For some reason he didn't want to think she had. Then he wondered if there was a special man in her life now. Don't be wondering about that, Tony, he told himself. That's none of your business, either.

He strained against the tool, causing the wire to stretch even tighter. "Your dad was a good teacher," he said.

Andrea nailed in the steeple, then looked up at him. "I wouldn't say this to just anyone, Tony. But I feel like I can tell you, because you knew how much I loved him. I was so angry at him when I'd discovered how he'd mortgaged the ranch. He was gone and I missed him terribly, but I was still angry."

"I think you had a right to be angry."

He loosened his grip on the wire cutter, then leaned against the fence post. Andrea noticed his denim shirt was already wet with sweat. Her eyes were drawn to his face and she was captured once again by its rough beauty.

At the moment he was looking at her and she could feel his gaze touch her cheeks, her lips and finally her eyes. Feeling very unsettled, she took a deep breath and said, "Yes, well, I kept saying to myself that it wasn't fair. But then I reminded myself of that old saying about the only fair being one with animals and exhibits."

His lips curved into a wry grin. "Like the one you came to Albuquerque to see," he said.

He shifted his back against the post and Andrea watched the muscles bulge in his arms as he folded them across his chest. "Why didn't you come to see me then? The ranch is only a few minutes' drive from the city."

Tony's question surprised her. She'd formed the impression that he wasn't all that pleased to see her. But then, as she'd observed earlier, his expression hadn't really told her all that much.

"I suppose because you never invited me, Tony."

His eyelids lowered a fraction. The look did strange things to Andrea's breathing.

"Would you have come if I'd asked you to?"

Why did she feel as if there were more to that question? "Yes, I would have," she answered simply.

He looked at her for another moment then pushed away from the post. "We'd better finish. It's getting darker."

They went back to the task of mending the sagging barbed wire. Yet Tony's question continued to nag at Andrea. After a few minutes had passed, she asked, "Tony, why haven't you ever asked me to come see you and the Rocking R?"

His hand plucked at the bottom string of barbed wire to test its tautness. For a moment Andrea thought he was going to ignore her question entirely.

Slowly he lifted his head. His expression had an aloofness about it that stung the soft part of her heart.

"We never did travel in the same circles, Andrea. We still don't."

The words cut her to the quick. "I didn't know you held that against me, Tony," she said in a small voice.

"I don't hold it against you. I'm merely stating a fact."

An unbearable lump had suddenly grown in Andrea's throat. She swallowed in an effort to relieve it.

"You were my friend, Tony. I never thought of my-self as any different from you."

His mouth curved wryly. "No, I know you didn't. But we *were* different. It wasn't anybody's fault."

Andrea struggled to take in the meaning of his words while Tony reached for the wire cutter lying in the dust at his feet.

She took a step forward, then stopped abruptly. "Tony, you still think of me as your friend, don't you?"

He straightened and looked at her as though her question had taken him by surprise. "Hell, Andrea," he muttered.

She was amazed at how important his feelings were to her. Expelling a pent-up breath, she said, "I—I know it's been a long time, but you've been with me all this time, Tony."

Andrea's words touched him in a place he hadn't known existed. All those years ago he'd been old enough and wise enough to realize that she'd had a crush on him. But he'd taken it for what it was—a young girl's crush. Being the foreman, and from a poor background, he figured she'd looked on him as forbidden so therefore more exciting. Tony had figured Andrea had put him out of her mind a long time ago. It did strange things to him to know that she hadn't.

"You never were too subtle, Andrea." He forced his voice to be light and his fingers to loosen their painful grip around the tool in his hands. "And, yes, I still think of you as my friend."

The smile that spread across her face dazzled him. For once, he knew the smile was just for him.

Lots of women had smiled at Tony Ramirez, but not women like Andrea. It proved to him that even though she had grown into a mature woman, Andrea still had not changed where he was concerned. Tony didn't know if that was a blessing or a curse.

"I'm glad," she said softly, then feeling a need to break the tension, she reached for the hammer. "You're right. It's getting darker. We'd better get this finished."

There were only two sections of fence remaining that needed repair. She and Tony worked quickly. While the two of them stretched and hammered, they talked of impersonal things like the weather and cattle prices. Andrea was curious as to how he liked living in New Mexico and asked him several things about the state. He surprised her by knowing much about New Mexican history and she enjoyed listening to his deep husky voice in the desert quietness.

"We'd better quit," Tony said after a few more minutes had passed. "It's getting too dark to see what we're doing, and we still have to walk back to the Jeep."

"We just have one more. Let's finish it so you won't have to make another trip out here," Andrea told him. "I think I can see well enough."

"Andrea—"

"Just stretch, Tony. Tomorrow you'll be glad we finished."

"I know I'd be wasting time to argue with you," he said, and reluctantly clamped the tool around the barbed wire.

Andrea didn't have any trouble starting the steeple into the wood with the first whack of the hammer, but the second one missed its mark and hit her squarely on the index finger.

"Ooh, darn! Ooh—"

The hammer fell from her hand and hit the ground with a thud. Andrea grabbed her injured finger.

"Damn it, I told you—"

"Shut up, Tony Ramirez. I'm all right—it's nothing."

Her words halted as he grabbed her hand. "Let me see it," he demanded.

"No! It's all right," she insisted. The pain made her voice wobble every so slightly. Andrea hoped he didn't notice. She'd never wanted Tony to think she was a soft socialite. She still didn't want him to think it.

Tony stabbed her with a threatening glare and began to peel her fingers away from the wounded one. "You know, Andrea, you could always talk me into things when—"

"It isn't your fault that I hit my finger," she interrupted.

"Yes it is," he said gruffly. "I should have never let you come out here—much less let you use the hammer—"

"Tony! Be quiet—"

Her whispered plea lifted his eyes from her finger up to her face, and Tony's heart lurched at what he saw there. Everything inside him told him to back away from her. But touching her, seeing her again after all this time had crumbled his resistance. Like a piece of forbidden fruit, he raised her injured finger to his mouth.

Something wild and wondrous began to build inside Andrea as he sucked on the aching finger. She wanted him. Wanted him with such sudden ferocity that it staggered her. She could think of nothing but his hard body, the sweaty earthy smell of him and the sweetness of his mouth.

Instinctively she swayed toward him and his arms reached for her. Once his hands closed around her waist, he pulled her tightly up against him and Andrea welcomed the hard crush of his body. Her face lifted, her lips parted in invitation.

The wondrous ache inside her burst and spread as his mouth closed over hers. Kissing Tony was like nothing she'd expected. It was swamping her, sucking her into some dark secret place where nothing existed but the two of them and this hot yearning slicing through the pit of her stomach.

Tony ended the embrace almost as quickly as it had begun. Without warning he jerked himself away from her and Andrea had to reach for the fence post to right herself. Her breath was coming hard and fast and she felt as if she'd been spun around quickly, then suddenly let go. It was a moment before she knew Tony was standing a few steps behind her.

She turned and found his back presented to her. Both his hands were curled into tight fists.

"What am I doing?" he muttered.

She reached out and touched his arm. He jerked away from her, then twisted around so that his eyes sliced through her.

"Tony—" she stammered in confusion. "I—"

"Don't do this," he said hoarsely. "Don't make me want you."

Bravely she took a step closer. "I wasn't trying to make you want me," she said, attempting to reason with him.

"No? Then I guess you were just trying to change my mind, to persuade me to help you," he said accusingly.

Andrea sucked in a harsh breath at his words. "Is that what you think? That I would stoop so low that— you conceited ass!"

His words had cut so deeply she could no longer bear the sight of him. Turning, she began to run. It was dark now and she could hardly see the terrain, but she didn't care. The pain of a fall wouldn't be nearly as bad as the emotion ripping through her.

"Andrea, come back!"

She ignored his call and went on to stumble over rock and cactus. She slid and scrambled to the bottom of the wash. Even in the darkness, Andrea could see that the palms of her hands were scraped and bleeding, yet she hardly noticed the discomfort.

Once she was back on her feet, she started in a run toward the road some fifty yards away. Tony's hand on her arm halted her steps before she crossed half the distance.

Desperately she tried to jerk away from him, but all she managed to do was make herself more breathless.

"What are you doing? Trying to kill yourself?"

She looked up at him, hoping to catch a glimpse of his face beneath the brim of his hat. "Trying to get away from you!" she said, gritting her teeth.

He drew closer and she could see the mocking twist of his lips. "You weren't trying to get away a moment ago," he said dryly.

Andrea felt her cheeks flaming in the desert night air. It was true that she had welcomed the embrace, but she hadn't been alone in that.

"Neither were you, Tony," she retorted angrily, "but I'm the one who was trying to seduce you, right? The young rich divorcée using her charms to gain favors, right? And all the time I'd been beguiled into thinking you were still my friend!"

"Andrea—"

"Oh, let's just forget it," she whispered in a wobbly voice. "It doesn't make any difference who was to blame. And anyway, you don't want to go back to El Paso and I—"

"Andrea, I didn't really mean that—what I said back there. It's just that—you're not like the women I know—you're..."

She could feel his fingers tighten on her arm. It reminded Andrea how passionately she'd reacted to his kiss. Her response to him confused her, but she reasoned that Tony was an attractive man and there were probably many women who would desire him. "Tony, don't set me apart from other women just because I've had money. I'm just a woman."

His hand left her arm and rose to her face. Andrea's breath seemed to stop as his fingers touched her cheek softly, sweetly.

"A beautiful woman," he murmured. "And you will always be different to me."

"Tony..." His name was all she could manage to whisper as his touch stole away her senses.

"And you weren't beguiled, Andrea. I do still think of you as my friend. You've been with me all this time, too."

Nothing could have eased the hurt inside her more than those words. She clutched them to her heart and gave him a shaky smile. "That's all that matters to me, Tony."

The corner of his mouth lifted to break the tautness of his features. "It's been a long time since I've seen the border. Maybe being a Texan again for a week wouldn't be so bad."

Andrea's eyes widened with surprise. "You mean—"

"I mean I'll go with you back to El Paso in the morning. But don't look to me for a miracle."

Andrea thought having him back home for a week was a miracle in itself. She suddenly wanted to shout with elation.

"Thank you, Tony. You'll never know how much this means to me."

He took a deep breath then reached for her arm. "Come on," he told her, moving in the direction of the road. "Let's get back to the house. There are plenty of things I need to take care of if we're going to leave in the morning."

As the two of them walked back to the Jeep, Tony wondered if he was the one who had just been beguiled.

Chapter Four

Andrea had been in bed at least an hour before she heard Tony retire to his room across the hall.

After they'd returned from fixing the fence, he had disappeared into the den to make several phone calls. Andrea had made herself scarce in order to give him privacy.

She'd taken a bath, washed her hair and dried it, then read a paperback she'd brought along with her. Even so, she was still keyed up and sleep seemed a long time away.

The night had cooled and the fan over her bed drew in air from the open windows. Through the parted curtains she could see the rising moon and the milky mass of stars strung across the desert sky.

It was very quiet here on the Rocking R. Much quieter than her ranch in El Paso, where muffled sounds of the city carried on the wind.

Andrea could hear each breath she took and every movement she made crackle the crisp sheets upon the bed. For some reason, seeing Tony again had awakened her senses, sharpened them to a keen awareness.

The rasp of a match being struck invaded the silence, then the smell of cigarette smoke filtered across to her. Obviously Tony wasn't asleep, either.

She rolled onto her side and closed her eyes. It was so easy to picture him lying against the white sheets, his dark hair rumpled, his body lean and brown and naked.

Andrea had felt so drawn to him out there on the dark mesa. She wondered why, and after thinking about it, she decided that seeing Tony again had been a bit like coming home. He represented a time in her life when she'd been young, carefree and happy. But the more she thought about it, the more she realized how closely Tony had been entwined in that happiness.

What did it mean? Sighing, she turned onto her back again and stared up at the ceiling. She thought back to that moment when he'd kissed her and she wondered what he'd been feeling.

Andrea was woman enough to know he'd been aroused. But had his reaction been purely sexual? Just the instinctive male arousal to a soft feminine body? No! She wouldn't believe that. She couldn't bear to think that any woman would have gotten the same response from him. She wanted to believe he'd responded because it was her. Because he felt something inside for her and only her.

Why would you want to believe that? she asked herself. Andrea told herself that she didn't know, then groaned as a voice inside her responded, *Yes you do!*

You love Tony. A part of you has always loved him. And you want, need for him to love you back!

The answering voice made Andrea go stock-still. She stared into the darkness and listened to the heavy thudding in her breast. Her heart seemed to be beating out an answer all its own, an answer that had been a long time in coming.

She forced herself to look back to when Tony had been on the ranch. He'd been such a big part of her days, her thoughts. She could see now that she had centered her life around him. There had always been a handy reason to be with Tony; cutting horses to be trained and exercised, cattle and fences to be checked on, odd chores around the stables.

Andrea had latched on to any reason to be with him simply because she'd wanted his company, she'd wanted to see him smile at her, she'd wanted to talk to him and tell him all the important and trivial things going on in her life. In return, she'd wanted to know all the things he'd been doing. She'd wanted to know what was important to him and then she'd set about planning how she could be a part of it.

Suddenly all that had ended. Tony had gone away. It was as if the world had stopped turning and all the meaning had gone out of Andrea's life. She'd lost her closest friend.

Andrea realized now, at this moment, that she'd been devastated because, even then, she must have loved Tony. She'd just been too young and immature to recognize the feeling for what it was. She'd always thought of him as a friend. Now her heart was telling her something altogether different.

What could she do about it? Tony had been very reluctant to spend one week in her presence. How could she expect to have more than that from him?

The telephone shattered the silence and pushed aside the question in her thoughts. Andrea wondered who would be calling so late at night. Rosita? Had something happened to Sara?

She started to climb from the bed and answer the ring when the sound stopped abruptly. After a moment she caught the husky sound of Tony's voice in the next room.

"I've already gone to bed," he said.

The caller must have made a reply because Tony chuckled in a lazy suggestive way.

Andrea stiffened upon the mattress as it suddenly dawned on her that he was speaking to a woman.

"Sorry about that," he went on. "I—had things to do this evening."

Andrea's fingers curled tightly against her palms. She had the urge to cover her ears but found that she could not make herself shut out his voice.

"You might as well mark me off. I'm leaving for El Paso tomorrow. I'll be gone a week."

She could hear him shifting in the bed. He was probably reaching to stub out his cigarette as he listened to the woman's comments.

"Business. Strictly business." He chuckled again. "Yeah. I'll call. As soon as I get back home."

The receiver clicked back into place. It was then Andrea realized she'd been practically holding her breath. She'd been so afraid she would hear him say something intimate and loving.

But he hadn't, and stale air rushed from Andrea's lungs as she rolled over and pressed her face into the pillow. She'd come to Tony for help, not to create more problems for herself. Yet now that these feelings for him had come to the surface, how did she ever expect to stop them? She wasn't even sure she wanted to.

Right now she was only going to think about tomorrow and the fact that he was going to El Paso with her. She held on to the thought, clutched it to her heart with fierce desperation. While he was there, she had to know, had to find out what he'd really been feeling when they'd kissed so passionately.

Andrea closed her eyes. Tomorrow she would be home and Tony would be there with her. It was the last thought she had before sleep finally claimed her.

"You won't have to worry about a thing," Zelda assured Tony the next morning.

Andrea smiled faintly as the woman poured fresh hot coffee for them.

"I know your husband will take care of things," he told her.

"Hmmph," Zelda snorted good-naturedly. "It won't be him who sees to things. It'll be me, and you know it."

Tony's lips quirked with a faint smile as he sliced into his pancakes. Andrea watched him from beneath her lashes. She was glad to see he wasn't in a dark mood this morning. She didn't think she could have made it through the long trip back to El Paso if he had been.

"It will only be for a week. I think everything will look after itself until then," he said.

Behind the kitchen table, Zelda plunged her hand into the sink full of dishwater. "How are the pancakes, Andrea?"

"Delicious," Andrea replied. "Although I'm trying not to think about all the calories I'm consuming."

Zelda made a disbelieving sound. Tony didn't seem to be taking any notice of their conversation.

"A lovely thing like you worrying about calories. If only I could be so blessed. I could eat a plate of those things three times a day and still look like this. Straight as a board."

Andrea laughed and Zelda went on, obviously curious about the other woman. "Rosita says you have a daughter. I wish you'd brought her with you. I never could have any kids. She sure would brighten up this place. I've given up on Tony ever marrying and having babies." She shrugged as though she'd long ago accepted Tony's bachelorhood. "Maybe next time you come you can bring her with you."

The statement made Andrea shift uncomfortably in her chair. Would Tony ever invite her back to the ranch? Somehow she doubted it. Six years had passed and he hadn't invited her. The idea hurt.

"I hardly ever get up this way. But perhaps sometime—" Her voice faded away. When she looked up from her plate, Tony was watching her. He obviously hadn't liked her reply. There was a faint frown pulling his black brows together. She did her best to ignore it and said, "Maybe you and your husband will be in El Paso sometime. I'd love for you to visit the ranch. Sara, my daughter, doesn't meet many strangers. And she loves company, especially if she can be the center of attention."

"I have a niece that lives in Las Cruces," Zelda said thoughtfully. "I might just come down sometime and visit you and my niece all in one trip." She looked from Andrea to Tony. "Tony's mother sure is fond of Sara. Every time she calls she talks about her, doesn't she, Tony?"

His face expressionless, he reached for his coffee cup. "Usually."

Andrea was surprised by this news. She had no idea that Rosita talked that much to Tony about Sara. Yet she should have known it, because Rosita often mentioned Tony in her conversations back on the Rio Vista.

Slicing into her pancakes, Andrea furtively studied the dark waves of his hair, the strong jut of his jaw and chin, the solid strength of his shoulders. She wondered if he'd ever asked his mother about her. She liked to think he had.

"Tony's parents are going to be very happy to see him," Andrea said.

Tony placed his coffee cup back on the table. "I imagine Mama will have all kinds of things cooked up for me. If I don't gain five pounds while I'm there it'll break her heart," he said fondly.

Zelda chuckled. "Then you'd better eat, Tony, because I don't want you breaking your mother's heart."

With a glint in his eyes, Tony looked across the table at Andrea, then glanced at Zelda.

"Andrea says that all the good-looking men have left El Paso. It isn't hard to figure out why she came up here after me, is it?"

Zelda threw back her head and laughed. "Tony, I'm sure once you heard about the problem you felt it your duty to let El Paso have you for a few days. But my Lord, what will they do when you have to leave?"

The question brought a deep laugh from Tony. Andrea watched him and Zelda and wished she could join in the merriment.

But it was impossible for Andrea to laugh when she put Zelda's question to herself. What would she do when Tony had to leave?

It was a warm beautiful morning when Tony and Andrea pulled away from the Rocking R. She gave the place one last look as Tony headed the car down the road that led them to the main highway.

Andrea had changed since she had arrived yesterday. She would never forget this place. In fact, she wanted to remember everything about it so that when Tony left her back in El Paso she could think of him and see him and his surroundings in her mind.

Yesterday she had wanted nothing more than for him to say he would help her. Today a tiny part of her wished that he had refused. It was going to hurt when the week was up and their time together ended.

She told herself not to think about it and looked across at his profile. He was concentrating on the road ahead of him. His left hand easily manipulated the steering wheel while his right rested loosely on the console between them. He was wearing a shirt of emerald green with a dull yellow thread running through it at even intervals. It made his hazel eyes appear vibrantly green.

Andrea was aware that the shirt, like his boots and the black leather belt studded with silver conchas at his waist, was an expensive item. That rich well-tailored look couldn't be found in chain stores. Those clothes wouldn't have been purchased on a foreman's salary, either.

Tony had never been a vain person, yet she wondered if he realized just how attractive he really was. His hair was one of his greatest assets. It was thick and glossy, the color of rich chocolate. Right now it was hidden by his black hat. But last night she had noticed the loose waves were carefully cut—not one of those hurried jobs with a pair of clippers. The back was just long enough to curl sexily over the edge of his collar.

She remembered how soft and silky it had felt when she'd thrust her fingers into it out there on the desert. Maybe the woman on the phone last night knew that feeling, too, she thought. Maybe she even knew what it was like to make love to him.

Sighing inwardly, Andrea forced her gaze back to the road. They had a long distance ahead of them. She couldn't be thinking along these lines. She had a ranch and a daughter to worry about. They had to come first.

"Zelda is a very nice woman. Has she worked for you long?"

He glanced her way. "Ever since I bought the ranch. She's very dedicated. And for some reason she likes me." He said this last with a little sheepish grin.

Andrea smiled knowingly. "No. She doesn't just like you. She dotes on you. But that isn't surprising. I remember you had collected a long list of girlfriends by the time I was in high school."

His black brows arched. "Now who told you that? Mama?"

She shook her head. "No. You did. Remember?"

One corner of his mouth curled upward. "I must have thought that would impress you." He glanced at her again. "Did it?"

Andrea laughed and the warm husky sound filled the interior of the car. "I was more impressed with the way you sat a saddle." *And your kindness, your gentleness, your hard work and tenacity,* she wanted to add.

He didn't say anything to that, and for a while they were both silent as the sports car rolled toward I-40.

Behind the wheel, Tony did his best to concentrate on his driving. It was very difficult when the car was so small, making the space between their shoulders a matter of inches.

Andrea was wearing another skirt this morning. It was shell pink and buttoned down the side. She had left three of the buttons undone and each time she shifted in the seat Tony imagined a bit more of her thigh was exposed to his gaze. Her fingernails were not long, yet had been painted a deep mauve color. There was a square-cut diamond on her right hand and a gold watch on her left wrist. He noticed that she wore no ring on her left hand. There wasn't even a faint tan line showing where one had been in the past.

As Tony studied her fingers he noticed they still had that tender graceful quality about them. He remembered last night, how soft and enticing they had felt when she touched him.

He'd never wanted a woman as badly as he had wanted her at that moment. Looking back on it now, he wondered where he'd found the strength to tear away from her. And looking at her here beside him now, he wondered where he was going to find the strength to stay away from her in the coming days.

Tony and Andrea made two stops. One at Socorro for gas and a snack and the last at a rest area just after they'd crossed into Texas. It was hot and the wind whipped the Lone Star flag that flew over the parking area. Tony stood in the shade of the building and waited while Andrea made use of the facilities.

The parking area was full of diesel rigs, tourists and travelers of all sorts. It had been a long time since Tony had been away from Albuquerque. Yet it did not feel strange at all to be back on highway 10, heading straight toward Mexico, toward El Paso, toward home.

Home. He still thought of El Paso as home even though it had been six years since he'd lived there. He wondered why he should feel that way. Then he knew why as Andrea appeared in the breezeway of the building.

Her heels clicked on the floor and he knew the men milling around them had their eyes on her. And why not? he asked himself. She was beautiful—even on the inside where it mattered the most.

As Andrea walked toward him, she smiled, just as she had always smiled at him. It made Tony feel good, and when she joined him he could not keep his hand from resting on the small of her back.

"Are you getting a breath of this good Texas air?" she asked, her cheeks dimpling up at him.

"You mean there's a difference?" he asked with mock innocence.

They started walking in the direction of the car and Andrea made a face at him. "Don't try to fool me, Antonio Ramirez. You're a Texan down to your soul."

His eyes clouded momentarily. "Some things change."

She shook her head. "Not things like that." She leaned over and tapped his chest with her finger. "Not things in here."

She flattened her palm against his heart and he looked at her quizzically. "I knew it!" she said. "I can feel it!"

"Feel what?"

"Your heartbeat. It's changed since we crossed the state line. I do believe that's a little Texas two-step beat."

He smiled, then realized she'd always been able to make him smile—even when he didn't want to.

"You are full of nonsense," he said, but his eyes were soft on her face.

"Come on now, Tony. Come on and admit it," she taunted, grinning at him. "Doesn't it feel good to see Texas again? Just a little?"

She measured her thumb and forefinger about an inch or two apart. "At least this much," she insisted.

He studied the space, then measured his fingers next to hers. His were a fraction closer together.

"I'd say about this much," he said.

She laughed with delight and gave his arm a shake. His glance caught hers and she was suddenly aware of the masculine muscles beneath her fingers. Their warmth evoked a soft quiver inside her. She wanted to hold on, to slide her fingers up his arm. Touch his shoulder, the hard intimate cords on his neck, the glossy brown hair brushing his dark skin.

Something flared in his eyes. Something that told Andrea he wanted to touch her, too. But by now they were at the car, and he pulled away from her to skirt around its hood and take his seat behind the wheel.

Andrea breathed deeply then climbed in beside him. For a moment back there they had smiled, joked and laughed. It had almost been as it used to be between them. Until they had touched. Touching Tony now was not like it had been six years ago. Now it was so intense, and it filled Andrea with an aching need to be physically close to him. She spent the next fifteen miles wondering what she could possibly do about it.

Chapter Five

The driveway leading to the Rio Vista ranch curved as it reached the house, then circled around to the back. Andrea had traveled over it hundreds of times, but now, with Tony beside her, she was aware of so much more. The richness, the beauty and the sense of what this place had meant to both of them filled her thoughts.

She looked across at him, trying to see by his expression if he was having similar feelings. It was difficult for Andrea to tell. Even though his expression remained blank, she knew his eyes were drinking in the surroundings. Inspecting or remembering?

He parked the car in front of the four-car garage. They were both climbing out on the ground when running footsteps sounded across the patio behind them.

"Mama! Mama!"

Two little brown arms wrapped around Andrea's legs. She straightened on her feet to greet her daughter. Tony watched intently as Andrea scooped the girl up in her arms. The child hugged her mother enthusiastically and Andrea laughed and kissed both her cheeks.

"Did you have fun, Mama? What did you see?" Sara asked.

Andrea set the child back on her feet. "Lots of things. I'll tell you all about them after supper. Now you tell me what you did."

Sara clung to her mother's hand and danced around on her little toes. "I rode the horse with Luis!"

"You did! How fun," Andrea responded. "Did Jenny get to come over and go swimming with you?"

The little girl nodded happily. "Rosita let us swim for two hours!"

Andrea laughed and patted her daughter's cheek. "You, young lady, are going to turn into a tadpole. Then I won't have a little girl anymore, I'll have a green frog."

Sara giggled loudly at her mother's teasing. Tony turned and unlocked the trunk of the car. The sight of Andrea's child affected him more than he'd thought it would. He couldn't imagine any man not cherishing Andrea and this child. If they belonged to him—no, Tony, don't even think it, he told himself with grim determination. Andrea has always been out of your league. Just be sure you keep remembering that.

By the time Tony had finished unloading the suitcases, Sara had noticed his presence. She walked boldly up to him and asked, "Who are you?"

His eyes squinting with amusement, Tony smiled down at her. "My name is Tony. What's yours?"

"Sara," she answered promptly, then gave him a gamine grin. "Is Rosita really your mama?"

He laughed. "She sure is. Why, don't you think I look like her?"

Sara giggled and tossed her dark ponytail back over her shoulder. Tony realized then that she was a perfect little replica of her mother. And just as enchanting.

"No! You look like Luis. Except you don't have wrinkles and gray hair."

Luis was Tony's father. He maintained the grounds and did all the minor and major fix-its around the place. He was a tall, thin man, very quiet. He had an ample portion of Irish mixed in with his Mexican blood, although it was not evident in his appearance, except for his height and his green eyes, both of which he had passed on to Tony.

Tony cocked an eyebrow at Andrea and she had to stifle a laugh.

"She's very observant," Andrea told him.

"Obviously," he said, his eyes settling back on the little girl. As Tony studied her small suntanned features, it suddenly struck him just how much Roy Rawlins had left behind and what a pitiful waste his dying had been. A pang of grief for his friend coursed through him in spite of his efforts to stem it.

"So are you the young lady who likes to ride horses?" he asked Sara.

The child nodded, her big blue eyes wide and curious as she studied this new visitor.

Tony stepped closer, a faint grin on his face. "Can you ride as well as your mama?" he asked.

Sara gave her little chin an indignant thrust. "Almost. But Mama sold my pony because he was getting too small."

"Maybe your pony wasn't getting too small, maybe you were getting too big?" Tony suggested.

After a moment or two of indecision, Sara gave him a reluctant shrug. "I guess so. I am getting big. Mama says I'm old enough to ride the big horses now."

"Is that so? Then I'm sure you're plenty big enough to ride on my shoulders. What do you think? Want a ride to the house?"

Sara took one look at Tony's smiling face and broad shoulders and nodded eagerly.

Tony's smile deepened and he reached to take the child in his arms. "Okay, up you go. Hold on to my neck real tight," he told her.

Sara obeyed and Tony began to gather some of the cases with one arm while Andrea picked up the last two.

They were almost to the house when Rosita came through the patio doors. She rushed up to Tony and kissed him on both sides of the face.

"Antonio," she breathed happily, stepping back to take a good look at him. "I knew you'd come. There wasn't a doubt in my mind. A son of mine could never refuse to help Andrea."

Tony thought of how close he'd come to doing just that. His mother never would have forgiven him for it. But on the other hand, he might never forgive himself for coming. In Albuquerque he could have kept a lid safely locked on his memories. Here in El Paso they were as fresh as a cactus rose, and Andrea was as vivid in them as she was here by his side.

"How are you, Mama?"

Rosita smiled smugly and turned around slowly for his inspection. She was wearing a red blouse and a full printed skirt with a white apron tied over it. She was beautiful to him in spite of her heavy form and graying hair.

"Beautiful and fat." He grinned at her. "Mama, if you keep eating like you do there is going to come a day when you won't be able to climb the stairs!"

Rosita cackled and patted him on the arm. Andrea smiled at the two of them. It was so good to see Rosita and Tony together. She knew how much the woman had missed her son since he'd gone away.

"Antonio, the day I have to quit eating is the day I won't care whether I climb the stairs or not."

"You're a terrible old woman," he told her with a wicked chuckle. "So where is Papa?"

"He's out working with the men. Something went wrong with the hay baler."

"Something serious?" Andrea asked anxiously.

Rosita turned to Andrea. "Don't start worrying, *chica*. It's nothing serious, just something to do with the baling wire."

The four of them started toward the house.

"It won't be long until supper," Rosita said as they walked. "Andrea, could you help Tony put his things away? He can sleep in the bedroom down from you. It has clean linen."

Tony opened his mouth to speak, then decided it would be best to wait until Sara wasn't present. How could his mother possibly expect him to stay in the same house with Andrea?

Grim-faced, he followed his mother through the sliding-glass doors at the back of the house. Once inside, he set Sara on her feet then turned to help Andrea with the bags.

He saw that Andrea was already climbing the staircase. Taking two stairs at a time, he caught up to her midway to the landing. Sara had gone with Rosita, so he knew no one could hear when he said, "Andrea, there is no use taking my things up the stairs. I can't stay here."

Andrea turned around to look at him and her brows lifted questioningly. "What do you mean? Where do you want to stay?"

"With Mama and Papa. I'm sure they have plenty of room since all my brothers are gone now."

She shook her head. "I'm sorry, Tony, I guess you didn't know. Rosita and Luis moved into the main house right after Dad died. We turned the storeroom into a place for them."

"What did you do with the house? Isn't it still there?"

Tony was speaking of the house his family had lived in when he was still here on the ranch. Since his parents had moved in with her, Andrea had turned the house into sleeping quarters for the hired hands. It worked out much better this way for everyone involved.

"It's still there. But I turned it into a bunkhouse."

His dark expression told her just what he thought of the news. Maybe he'd been more attached to the old place than she'd realized.

"Then I'll stay in the bunkhouse with the men."

Andrea frowned at him, then turned and started to mount the stairs. "You will do no such thing, Tony! It's not nearly as comfortable out there."

"I don't need comfort," he said shortly.

Confused by his attitude, she turned to look at him once again. "Maybe you don't need it," she said. "But I don't want you to stay out there with a bunch of men you don't even know. I want you to stay here in the house."

"I've never stayed in this house before. It wouldn't be right to stay in it now—with you."

Tony hadn't meant to be so abrupt. He could see that she was hurt by what he'd said. Damn, this was going to be harder than he thought.

Andrea's chin dropped as she turned to climb up and away from him. His words had wounded her. She hoped he couldn't detect it in her voice. "Then don't think of it as staying with me. Think of it as staying with your parents. They live here, too, you know."

Sighing with exasperation, Tony followed her. "Andrea, you're not listening to me!"

She glanced at him over her shoulder. "No, Tony, I'm not. I don't want to argue with you over this—it's senseless."

Andrea turned the corner at the landing. Tony's cowboy boots treaded with light quick steps just behind her.

By the time she reached the bedroom door, Tony caught her by the arm. Andrea looked straight up into his troubled green eyes.

Yes, it was senseless all right, Tony silently agreed as he looked upon her face. It had been senseless to think he could come down here and remain indifferent to her. "Do you know what it will cost me to stay here? To know that you are only a few steps away? I'm not made of iron."

Was he admitting that he was attracted to her? A desperate quiver invaded her body. Her eyes clung to his. "Maybe I do know, Tony. Maybe it will cost me just as much."

He drew his breath in and turned away from her. "I should have never come here," he said hoarsely.

"But you have," she told him quietly. "And you belong here in the house with me and Sara, with your parents. Not with the hired hands! You're a part of the family, Tony. A part of me."

He swallowed, then looked at her with an oddly detached expression. He'd never expected to hear Andrea say something like that. He wasn't sure he wanted her to.

"I guess I still think of myself as your dad's hired hand," he said with a wry twist to his mouth.

She smiled with gentle understanding. "Yes, I guess this house does bring it all back to you. But that was a long time ago, Tony, and things are different now."

His hand was still on her arm. Tony realized he didn't want to take it away. She felt warm and soft and the light in her eyes pulled at him.

"Are they really different, Andrea?"

She reached for his hand. It felt big and rough and strong against her fingers. To touch it was comforting as well as disturbing.

"We've both had changes in our lives." The curve of her mouth deepened, dimpling her cheeks. "And we've both grown older. Things *are* different now. But you know, just because our lives have changed doesn't mean good things can't happen. Good things are already happening—because you're here."

Andrea's words touched him in a place that he'd meant to keep hidden. It left him feeling helpless and hopeless to know she could pierce his defenses with just a word, just a touch.

By the end of seven days, if he wasn't careful, Andrea would be holding him in the palm of her hand. Tony couldn't allow that. Because in the end, he didn't want either of them to be hurt. And that was exactly what would happen if he let himself become involved with her.

"Rosita, can you hold off dinner a little while? I'd like to take Tony down to meet the men."

The older woman glanced up from the boiling pot to see Andrea's face peering over the bat-wing doors of the kitchen. A broad smile split her dark face. "For you and Tony—thirty-five minutes. But no longer."

"We'll be here," Andrea informed her happily, then disappeared to go find Tony.

He was at the stables—just the place Andrea figured he would be. Other than Tony, she supposed there was no one who loved horses more than she did. Except maybe her daughter, Sara.

Stabled at one end was a pretty sorrel gelding she'd purchased not more than a year ago. Tony was presently inspecting him while the horse was nuzzling and searching for the hidden sugar cubes Andrea usually spoiled him with.

A surge of warm pleasure filled her as she approached Tony. They had once had so much fun riding together. She hoped they would have the chance to ride again before he went back to Albuquerque.

"I see you have found Odds Maker. What do you think of him?"

"Odds Maker?" he repeated with skepticism. "Have you been racing him?"

She chuckled softly and leaned against the stall just inches away from him and the horse's nose. "No.

When I purchased him he'd been on the track a few times. But I certainly can't afford to be in the horse-racing business now.''

He stroked the sorrel's neck. "He's a pretty thing," he said. "And he looks like something you'd buy. Strong and leggy. Do the men use him, or is he just your pleasure?''

"I let the guys use him if they have to have an extra mount. But he's usually my darling." Her voice softened on the last words. She reached over and fondled the horse's velvety muzzle. He muzzled her hand and she said, "No sugar this time, Odds Maker. I came down here to see Tony, not you.''

She stroked the sorrel's neck with obvious affection, then cast Tony a rueful glance. "He was a little flighty when I first got him. He lost me the second time I rode him.''

Tony chuckled at her admission. "I'm sure that hurt your pride.''

She grimaced. "My pride and a few other things," she added wryly. "But Odds Maker and I understand each other now.''

Her eyes still on Tony, she smiled and rested her cheek against the horse's neck. "I'd like you to ride with me before you have to leave. I want to show you how Odds Maker can fly. I've never had a horse so fast!''

His lips quirked with a faint smile. He didn't think it would be wise for them to go riding. Yet he knew he could not refuse her that much. To be honest, Tony didn't want to refuse himself the chance to be with her again.

"You're probably exaggerating," he said. "I'll have to see it to believe it.''

Andrea laughed with pleasure. "Just don't blink your eyes, Tony, or you may miss me when I pass you."

Tony joined her laughter and she pushed herself away from the stall door and latched on to his arm. "Come on. I thought we would go down to where the men are working with the hay. You can see your father and meet the other men."

Tony did his best to ignore her gentle touch as they strolled beneath the long shedrow. He couldn't let himself believe it was any more than a casual touch. So why did it feel like so much more? Why couldn't he remember that this woman was that same girl who'd been off limits to him six years ago?

Andrea had changed her dress clothes for a pair of faded jeans and a plum-colored shirt. Both were well-worn and clung to her curves like a soft glove. Her gray cowboy boots sent up little puffs of dust as she matched her stride with his.

Tony noticed the sun setting on her face, the pink and magenta hues shading her cheeks and lips. She was like a piece of ripe fruit. And Tony realized he'd never been so hungry. Forbidden or not, he wanted to taste her. But he knew that one taste would only leave him craving another.

The two of them climbed into one of the old pickups they used on the ranch, and Tony drove them out to the hay field.

When they arrived, the men were just starting up the hay baler and Luis was climbing into his truck to head back to the main house.

Andrea waved and signaled to him. Luis quickly got out of the truck and loped over to them.

Several of the workers were surprised to see Luis embrace the young man who'd arrived with the boss lady.

Moments later Andrea asked Luis, "Isn't it good to see Tony on the Rio Vista again?" Her face was beaming as brightly as Luis's.

"It's damn good," Luis said, giving his son's shoulder a sound shake.

"Andrea asked me to come," Tony told his father.

"None too soon, either. We need you here, *niño*. But then I guess she's told you that."

Tony nodded. "I'll do what I can."

Luis smiled encouragingly and gave Tony's shoulder another shake. "That'll be enough, son." He glanced over at Andrea. "Has Mama got supper ready?"

Luis had always called Rosita "Mama." In all the years she'd known them, Andrea had never heard him call her by any other name.

Andrea nodded. "She's waiting for us to return. I'm just going to introduce Tony to the men. We'll be up in a few minutes."

He nodded, told Tony how good it was to see him once again, then left.

Several yards away, five men had gathered around a water can situated on a tailgate. Tony could feel the men sizing him up and knew they were watching Andrea as she reached for his hand and clasped her fingers around it.

"Guys, this is Tony Ramirez, Luis's son from Albuquerque. Tony, this is Peter Burns, Jay Lopez, Windell McCurry, Steven Logan and my foreman, Larry Baker."

All the men nodded and said hello. Tony did like-
wise while letting his eyes linger on the last man. He
was, Tony suspected, nearing forty. Short sandy-
colored hair jutted in straight tufts beneath his straw
hat. He had a rusty-red mustache and milky-gray eyes.
Tony disliked him instantly.

"Tony's going to be staying a few days, so you'll
probably be seeing him around. He's also going to be
advising me about the ranch, so if he asks for anything or can use any kind of help from you men, I
expect you to follow his orders. Okay?"

They all voiced their compliance—all except the
foreman. Tony noticed he was watching Andrea beneath lowered eyelids. Tony met his gaze with a determined glint that told the foreman in no uncertain
terms that he would not tolerate anything out of the
ordinary.

"Say, weren't you the foreman here? A long time
ago?" Steve, one of the younger men, asked.

Tony looked at him with surprise. "Yes. I was."

Andrea smiled at Tony. "See? Your reputation pre-
cedes you."

"Yeah, I've heard some of the older men talk about
you," Windell said. "Said you were a hell of a horse-
man. Maybe you could give us some pointers on that
filly Ms. Rawlins is fond of."

"I'll try," he told the younger man. Frankly Tony
was surprised that anyone had heard of him. He'd
been in Albuquerque for a long time now, and several
foremen had worked on the Rio Vista after him.
Maybe Tony had meant something to this place after
all.

"I guess you knew Roy Rawlins."

This was from the current foreman and Tony turned to look at him. "That's right. I did know him."

"I guess you knew Andrea then, too?"

Some of the men shifted uncomfortably at the annoyed expression on Tony's face.

"That's right," Tony repeated coolly. He didn't like the man using Andrea's first name. It wasn't that they were formal around here; it was more that the man had done it in a disrespectful way, as if to imply he knew Andrea in a personal way and wanted Tony to know it.

Tony's teeth ground together. No man in the whole of El Paso knew Andrea the way he did!

Andrea smiled up at Tony and spoke quickly in an effort to dispel the sudden tension flaring between the two men. "Tony and I have known each other for a long time."

"Yes," he agreed. He smiled at her, unaware of the intimate look in his eyes.

Andrea, however, did notice his expression. It made her feel warm and cared for. And she realized that Tony's being back on the ranch was making everything look different—better.

Tony spoke to the men for a few more minutes, telling them what he would be doing and looking for in the next few days. It was growing dark when the two of them finally left the hay field.

"What do you think of the men?" she asked as they headed back to the main house.

He looked across the seat at her. She had rolled down the window and the breeze was whipping her dark hair. "They seem fine, except for the foreman. I think you need to let him go."

Andrea sat straight up in the seat. "Let him go?" she repeated. "Just like that?"

He merely shrugged in reply and Andrea let out an impatient breath. "Tony, come on! The man hasn't actually done anything to warrant being fired. Besides, you're only going to be here a week. That's hardly time to find a replacement."

"So? You wouldn't be losing anything if you got rid of him."

Her eyes widened in surprise. "I can't believe you. How can you tell he's no good after just a few minutes? You're letting what I told you earlier sway your judgment."

"He called you Andrea," he said between gritted teeth. "I wanted to bust him in the mouth."

Andrea laughed in disbelief. "That *is* my name, Tony."

The pickup jostled over a rough spot in the road. Tony kept his eyes on the track in front of him. "He's only the foreman. He has no right to call you by your first name!"

Andrea had to smile inwardly at his words. She couldn't believe he was making an issue over such a little thing. "You called me Andrea when you were the foreman," she reminded him.

His eyes cut her way. "That was different."

Her brows lifted questioningly. "Oh?"

"You didn't own the ranch then."

"That's true," she conceded.

"Andrea, the man has no breeding, no manners. He treats you with disrespect."

"I didn't hire him for his social graces."

He snorted angrily. "You wanted my advice so I'm giving it. He's no good, Andrea."

She looked away from him and out the window. "You're probably right," she said. "I've never felt fully satisfied with him, but he's an improvement over the last one. And he keeps the men working. Besides, this is the man's only livelihood. I'd hate to suddenly take it away from him without any notice."

Andrea's response didn't surprise Tony. She'd always had a soft heart. But Tony had discovered a long time ago that you couldn't survive in this world with a soft heart.

"Okay, then," he said, relenting against his better judgment. "I'll watch him while I'm here. If he doesn't show me anything to change my mind, then I believe you should consider finding someone to replace him."

"That's fair enough," she said.

He didn't say anything, and after a moment Andrea glanced at him and said, "I guess you think I'm being stubborn about this."

His grin was crooked. "I think you are being just like the Andrea I used to know."

"Is that good or bad?"

It was nice to hear his chuckle.

"A little bit of both," he said.

By now they were back at the barns and stables. Tony parked the truck and they started up the sloping grounds that led to the back of the house.

The air had grown cool with the sinking of the sun. Night was falling over the desert mountains with a hush. For the first time in a long time Andrea felt a sense of contentment as she and Tony walked side by side, their shoulders separated by mere inches.

"Your mother has cooked something special for you tonight, just as you predicted she would," she told him.

His teeth flashed in the dark. "She knew I would come, didn't she?"

Andrea nodded. "She assured me from the very beginning that if I asked you, you'd come."

"And what about you, Andrea, did you think I would?"

She thought about his question for a moment. "I didn't know, Tony. But I wanted you to."

They'd reached the fence that enclosed the back-yard. Before Tony opened the gate, he turned and looked back at the stables and barn and the wide expanse of pastureland behind them. "The ranch is just as beautiful as I remembered it," he mused aloud. To himself he added, *And so are you, Andrea.*

Chapter Six

As Andrea had predicted, dinner was a big affair. Most of the conversation was between Tony and his parents with Sara making comments whenever she had the chance.

Now that Andrea was a mother, she knew what it meant to Rosita and Luis to have their son with them. It gave her a good feeling to watch them eating and talking together, laughing and reminiscing. Even though the ranch was in trouble, tonight Andrea felt good and warm inside.

After the food and dishes were cleared away, they all went outside into the courtyard to enjoy the fresh air. Andrea allowed Sara to swim while the grown-ups drank their after-dinner coffee at the poolside.

Andrea noticed that Tony was watching Sara as she played and splashed in the water. She wondered if Tony wanted children...if he'd ever met a woman he'd like to have a child with. It was easy for her to picture

Tony being a father, but it wasn't quite so easy to think of him with another woman.

It was growing late when Andrea finally coaxed Sara out of the pool and into the house to get ready for bed. The little girl had already told the grown-ups good-night and was headed through the patio doors when she suddenly bolted around her mother's legs and ran back out to Tony's chair.

Sara looked up at him with great seriousness and asked, "Are you going to take me riding?"

Tony glanced over at Andrea and the two of them exchanged a knowing look.

"I'll take you riding if your mother says you can go. Would you like to go riding?"

Sara tapped her little toe out in front of her and wrinkled her face in contemplation. Tony knew he was lost when she rolled her big blue eyes up at him. "Maybe," she hedged, "if I could ride on the front of the saddle with you."

"Sara!" Rosita scolded. "You're a big girl. You can ride all by yourself now."

Sara looked across at Tony's mother. "No I can't! The horses are all too tall and scary. If I rode with Tony he wouldn't let me fall. Besides, Tony is nice!"

Before Tony had time to be surprised, Sara had leaned over and kissed him on the cheek then sped across the patio to her mother. Rosita and Luis chuckled heartily as Andrea quickly ushered Sara inside.

While helping Sara to bed, Andrea hoped Tony realized that little girls were just like big ones when it came to a man's charms.

"Do you like Tony?" she asked her daughter as she tucked the clean sheet under Sara's chin.

Sara nodded enthusiastically. "Do you think he likes me?"

"I'm sure he does," she assured Sara. "He told you he would take you riding."

The child made a glum face. "Yes. but I had to ask him to."

Andrea had to smile at her daughter's reasoning. "I'm sure Tony would have asked you sooner or later."

"Does Tony have a little girl?" Sara asked suddenly.

Andrea shook her head and touched the tip of Sara's nose with her finger. "No. He doesn't have a little boy or a little girl. So while he's here I want you to show him how nice you can be."

"Tony would make a nice daddy, don't you think, Mama? I'd like to have a daddy like him."

Sara's words took her completely off guard, but as they sank in, emotion swelled within Andrea.

"Yes, darling. Tony is a very nice man. He would be a good daddy. But you can't just pick a daddy out like you do a new dress."

Sara's little lips turned down at the corners and she folded her hands primly on top of the sheet. "My real daddy is gone. Does that mean I'll never have another one?"

At this moment Andrea could have explained many things to her daughter. But somehow she didn't think the time was right for either of them. Instead, she said simply, "No, it doesn't mean you'll never have one. So go to sleep now and tomorrow we'll do something fun together."

Her words seemed to satisfy Sara. When Andrea kissed her good-night and closed the bedroom door there was a smile on her sweet little face.

Back downstairs, Andrea placed a decanter of wine on a tray beside four goblets. When she reached the poolside, she found Tony alone, smoking a cigarette.

"Where are Rosita and Luis?"

"They decided to retire for the night."

"I thought they'd stay up later tonight since you were here," she said.

He shrugged and then his lips slanted in a faint smile. "And they thought I wanted to be alone with you."

The surprise on her face was hidden as she placed the tray on a low table between the webbed lawn chairs. "Did you? Do you?"

He pulled the cigarette from his mouth then stubbed it out. "Why do you always put me on the spot, Andrea?" he asked jokingly. "Do you know you always did that to me in the past?"

His teasing tone lightened the moment. She smiled at him and continued to pour a small amount of wine into two of the glasses. "I think," she said, handing him one of the glasses, "that you remember too much about my bad habits."

She sank into the chair next to him and took a sip of her wine. He watched her through hooded eyes and remembered how she had always tagged along by his side.

Seeing her now in the darkness, her hair loose and tumbling against her back, her gaze on the burning stars overhead, he knew she had, in a roundabout way, caused his life to take a different path.

...be tempted!

See inside for special
4 FREE BOOKS offer

Discover deliciously different romance with 4 Free Novels from

Silhouette Romance™

Sit back and enjoy four exciting romances—yours **FREE** from Silhouette Books! But wait . . . there's *even more* to this great offer! You'll also get . . .

A USEFUL, PRACTICAL DIGITAL CLOCK/ CALENDAR—FREE! As a free gift simply to thank you for accepting four free books we'll send you a stylish digital quartz clock/calendar—a handsome addition to any decor! The changeable, month-at-a-glance calendar pops out, and may be replaced with a favorite photograph.

PLUS A FREE MYSTERY GIFT—A surprise bonus that will delight you!

You can get all this just for trying Silhouette Romance!

FREE HOME DELIVERY

Once you receive your 4 FREE books and gifts, you'll be able to preview more great romance reading in the convenience of your own home. Every month we'll deliver 6 brand-new Silhouette Romance novels right to your door months before they appear at retail. If you decide to keep them, they'll be yours for only $1.95 each*—with no additional charges for home delivery!

SPECIAL EXTRAS—FREE

You'll also get our monthly newsletter, packed with news of your favorite authors and upcoming books—FREE! And as a valued reader, when you join our Reader Service, we'll be sending you additional free gifts from time to time—as a token of our appreciation.

BE TEMPTED! COMPLETE, DETACH AND MAIL YOUR POSTPAID ORDER CARD TODAY AND RECEIVE 4 FREE BOOKS, A DIGITAL CLOCK/CALENDAR AND A MYSTERY GIFT—PLUS LOTS MORE WHEN YOU JOIN OUR READER SERVICE!

* Terms and prices subject to change.

A FREE DIGITAL CLOCK/ CALENDAR
and Mystery Gift await you, too!

✓ Clip and mail this postpaid card today!

Silhouette Romance™

Silhouette Books®
901 Fuhrmann Blvd., P.O. Box 1867, Buffalo, NY 14240-9952

☐ **YES!** Please rush me my four Silhouette Romance novels with my FREE Digital Clock/Calendar and Mystery Gift, as explained on the opposite page. I understand that I am under no obligation to purchase any books. The free books and gifts remain mine to keep. If I choose to continue in the Reader Service, I'll receive 6 books each month as explained on the opposite page. I can cancel at any time by dropping you a line or returning a shipment at your cost.

215 CIL HAX2

NAME _____
(please print)

ADDRESS _____ APT. _____

CITY _____ STATE _____ ZIP _____

Offer limited to one per household and not valid to current Silhouette Romance subscribers. Prices subject to change.

Clip and mail this Postpaid Card today! ⌄

BUSINESS REPLY CARD

First Class   Permit No. 717   Buffalo, NY

Postage will be paid by addressee

SILHOUETTE BOOKS
901 Fuhrmann Blvd.
P.O. Box 1867
Buffalo, NY 14240-9952

NO POSTAGE
NECESSARY
IF MAILED
IN THE
UNITED STATES

"The stars look different here than they did on the Rocking R," she mused.

He followed her gaze. "They're the same."

"But they don't seem the same," she said.

"Different places make us feel differently about things."

That was very true, she thought. She swallowed a bit more of the wine and looked at him. It was quite dark now, but a faint light coming from the house illuminated his profile.

She let her eyes become her fingers as they touched the indentation in his chin, then slid up to the hard male line of his lips. Only twenty-four hours ago they had stood out under these same stars, held each other, kissed each other passionately. The heat of that moment was still alive within her. Even as she looked at him now, yearning sliced through her like lightning slicing through a black sky—jagged, powerful and totally merciless.

"Do you have a girlfriend?"

Andrea didn't know if she was drunk from his presence or the wine. One of the two must have made her ask the question.

He looked at her, his mouth twisting mockingly. "What makes you ask?"

She wanted to look away from him, but his eyes had always been magnetic. They held her gaze and brought a strange heat to her face.

"Just being a woman, I suppose. And the fact that I overheard you talking to someone last night."

One of his dark brows lifted and a raspy chuckle passed his lips. "So you could tell it was a woman?"

She grimaced. "I'd hate to think you'd talk to a man that way."

He wondered if she hated hearing him talk to a woman that way, then told himself to forget the question. "You're right. It was a woman. But not a girlfriend."

Her brows arched suspiciously. She knew he could be a charmer when he wanted to be. A woman wouldn't stand much of a chance if Tony Ramirez decided to go after her. It hurt to know he would never woo her.

"Sara is smitten with you," she told him. "And I— I wanted to thank you for being so understanding with her."

"She's a wonderful child." He took a sip of wine and slanted her a look. "Does her father ever visit her?"

Andrea shook her head. "He wasn't interested in being a father. Once we got divorced, he broke contact completely. I think he lives on the West Coast now."

Tony was glad to hear she had no remaining connection to her ex-husband. But then he was angry at himself for being glad. It shouldn't matter, he told himself. But it did.

"Well, maybe it won't always be that way," he said. "I mean, maybe in time you'll find a man who would be a good father to Sara and a good husband to you."

Everything inside Andrea tightened at his words. She didn't need to look for a man. She had already found him. But how could Tony know that? How could he know that he was the man she'd really been waiting for all her life? Andrea had just discovered the truth herself. How could she possibly explain how she felt to Tony? Before he left to go back to Albuquerque, she had to find a way to tell him.

"It would be nice to have someone—to love. But I haven't been looking," she said quietly.

Relief poured through him and Tony cursed himself for it. "I'm prying. Tell me not to pry, Andrea."

She smiled faintly and gripped the stem of her wineglass. "I want to talk with you about me, about you, about everything. We could always talk to each other before."

Tony drained off the last of his wine and placed his glass on the low table between them. The tension surrounding them was almost visible. He could practically taste it as it mingled with the words on his tongue. He knew he should speak but found he was afraid to. He was afraid he might say how much he'd like to take her in his arms and kiss her soft mouth again.

He'd heard that to love someone you had to first be their friend. Well, he'd known Andrea as a friend. Now he wanted to know her as a lover. Last night she'd kissed him. But last night she'd probably been feeling alone and desperate, he decided. Andrea could have her pick of men. Why would she look at someone like him?

His conflicting thoughts had him reaching to his pocket for another cigarette. Rising to his feet, he said, "It's late. I think I'll go up to bed."

Andrea watched him bring the match flame to the end of the cigarette and realized that she was disappointed. She wanted his company. Even if he didn't say another word, she still wanted to know that he was beside her in the darkness.

"It's not that late, Tony, and the night is so beautiful. Won't you walk with me?"

She stood and looked at him questioningly. Tony pulled the cigarette from his lips. "If you really want me to."

She smiled and reached for his hand. "I do. We can walk down the front drive. The cannas are in full bloom now. So are the yuccas, and the moon shines bright enough to see them."

They walked around the house and started down the graveled drive. Andrea thought once again how good his hand felt in hers and how satisfying such a simple touch could be.

"I think there's no place like the border," she sighed as they strolled along, taking in the flowers and the soft night sounds. "It's a place where people with different cultures and different lives merge and live together. Both governments see the border as a problem, I suppose, but I've always thought of it as fascinating."

"The fall of the peso has made it tough on everyone," Tony commented.

She nodded and looked up at him. "Have you missed the border, Tony? Have you ever wanted to come back?"

His eyes filled with the beautiful lines of her face. He ached to kiss her and wondered if seeing her again had cast some kind of powerful spell over him.

"At first I missed it," he admitted. "But then I became so busy with the Rocking R that I didn't have much time to think about it."

"Did you ever think of me, Tony?"

"Andrea," he groaned, and tugged her along.

"Well, did you?" she persisted.

The frown on his face was suddenly replaced by a wry grin. "Here you go again," he told her. "I still remember that time you came up to me at your birthday party and asked me to dance. Then you quickly went on to ask me if I thought you looked pretty."

Andrea laughed deeply. "I did do that, didn't I?"

It should have embarrassed her that he remembered, but instead it pleased her.

"I never knew what to expect from you." He still didn't, he realized. "But to answer your question, of course I thought of you. I thought of everyone back here."

Andrea had meant in a more personal way. But she forced herself to be content with his answer. "I thought about you, Tony. I thought about you a lot."

He didn't say anything. Andrea searched his profile in the darkness. What was behind those beautiful hazel eyes of his? Did he care that he'd been in her thoughts?

"You must have missed all that teasing."

Her smile was touched with a hint of sadness. "That and more."

Tony felt that the conversation was inching toward dangerous ground. He knew he should play it light. But something about the sound of her voice, the touch of her hand, compelled him to go on. "Less than a year after I left the ranch, you married."

Andrea's throat tightened and she took a deep breath. "Yes, I did. It was a terrible mistake. I realize now that I married him on the rebound. That never works."

His hand pulled on hers, forcing her to halt her steps. "I don't understand. Did someone hurt you?"

Andrea hardly knew she was gripping his fingers. She was too caught up in his searching gaze. "Yes. You did, Tony."

He went utterly still and Andrea knew she had shocked him.

"Andrea," he began slowly. "That can't be true. We weren't—we were—"

"Just friends," she finished for him. "Yes, we were friends. But to me you were so much more. I guess you didn't know that."

He let go of her hand and curled both of his over her shoulders. "I knew that at one time you had a crush on me. But that's—"

Andrea's eyes dropped from his face and focused on the V on his shirt. For dinner he had changed the emerald shirt for a white one. His skin gleamed like rich oak beside the light cotton fabric. She longed to lean forward and press her lips against it, to taste its warm sweetness.

"As a young teenager I did have a crush on you," she admitted. "I was just becoming aware of what the word *man* really implied. Just one look at you made my heart go pitter-pat."

Tony had to smile at that. "There were other men around, Andrea."

She smiled tentatively back at him. "I told you all the good-looking men had left El Paso. That happened when you left."

A husky laugh gurgled in his throat. "Andrea, you're trying to flatter me."

"You don't need flattery, Tony. You already know what you are."

His dark brows arched. "I'm a poor Mexican. That's all I've ever been."

"That's ridiculous. You're not poor."

"Compared to you, I am."

Letting that last comment slide, she said, "God gave you some things a lot of rich men would like to have."

"I'm glad of that, because I damn sure have had to work for everything else," he said.

"You've never been bitter about coming from a poor background, have you?"

He shook his head. "That would be like being bitter over not having enough sunshine or enough rain. Bitterness is a wasteful emotion."

And Tony had never been wasteful; Andrea was certain of that. He'd taken everything he'd owned and poured it into the Rocking R in order to make something for himself. He was intelligent, talented and possessed enough looks to kill, but still he considered himself poor. Andrea wondered why that was.

"I've never thought of you as poor, Tony," she said.

He slid his hands down from her shoulders and grasped both her hands. "You should have," he told her, his face carefully guarded. "And I think we should go back now. It's getting late."

He pulled on her hands, but she held her ground. "Wait. Tony, I—"

Tony looked down at her and Andrea's heart began to thud heavily, painfully. She'd never had it react so violently to one man's look, one man's touch.

"I meant what I told you earlier," she went on. "Maybe you don't believe me. But I did marry on the rebound. I was very hurt when you went away. I couldn't understand why you went. I thought—I thought that maybe—" She closed her eyes and swallowed. "I was falling in love with you, Tony."

"Andrea, you were very young and—"

Her eyelids lifted and she gazed at him through the silky veil of her lashes. "I didn't care about anything for a long time after you left. Tony, why did you go? I was beginning to think you cared for me. I mean, really cared for me. And then the next thing I knew you were gone."

He was silent for a long time. Andrea could feel every nerve inside her coiling tighter and tighter as she waited for him to answer.

"There were many reasons why I left," he said finally.

The desert breeze had blown her dark hair into her eyes, but Andrea didn't bother to push it away. She didn't want to let go of his hands and lose the magic of his touch.

"I used to lie awake at night trying to think of at least one," she told him, "and now you tell me there were many. I don't understand, Tony. I didn't then. I don't now."

"I had grown out of the foreman's job. I wanted more."

"I can understand that. So why couldn't you have come to me and told me that?" she asked. Then her eyes dropped from his and a rueful expression spread across her face. "Or maybe I didn't even mean enough to you to deserve a goodbye. That's what I've believed all these years."

"Oh, Andrea, that's not true."

"It happened."

"Hell, Andrea, if I'd thought you were going to cross-examine me, I would have never come—"

"Why can't you tell me, Tony?" she asked, unaware of the jut of her chin, the quiver of her lips.

Tony noticed though, and it was all he could do to keep from drawing her up to him, kissing her lips until the quiver was gone, till her soft body was melting against his.

"Okay, Andrea, you want the main reason, I'll give it to you," he said. "Roy came to me and asked me to leave."

"Dad!" His words were like a sharp slap in the face. "But why? You and he were always good friends!"

He shrugged and one corner of his mouth lifted in a dry sort of smile. "I guess that's why he felt he could come to me, because I was his friend. Because he figured I would understand his motives."

"What motives?" she asked in confusion, her eyes darting across his face, searching for answers.

"You, Andrea. He thought you were getting too attached to me. He wanted you to turn your interest to younger men, men more your own age and your own class. In other words, he wasn't about to let his daughter fall for a poor Mexican, foreman or not."

"And what did you think, Tony?"

Tony dropped his hold on her hands and stepped away from her. He'd left his hat back at the house and Andrea watched him push his lean fingers through the silky waves of his dark hair.

"I thought he was overreacting," he said. "So you had a crush on me. I knew it would pass once you grew older and saw me as I really was."

Andrea ignored his last disparaging remark and stepped closer to him. "If you were so certain of that, why didn't you explain that to my father? Why did you just agree and go?"

"Andrea, it was all a long time ago. It shouldn't matter now."

"But it does matter!" she countered. "Maybe you don't think a young woman's feelings are that important, but they can be hurt, too."

"I said I was sure of you," he said, his voice rough with frustration. "But I wasn't sure of myself, Andrea. I was attracted to you. And I knew that attraction could become a real problem. You were like a beautiful tempting diamond to someone who'd known little more than dusty cow lots and girls who waded across the river. It seemed safer and saner to go and not be tempted."

Andrea let out a deep sigh. She suddenly felt very tired and very sad. "I guess neither one of us understood what was going on."

Tony didn't quite know what she meant by that statement. But he did want her to understand one thing. "I never meant to hurt you, Andrea. I never, ever wanted to hurt you. Can you believe that?"

Andrea raised her head and nodded. "Yes, I believe you," she said quietly. "Your coming down here to help me proves that much."

Tony didn't reply. There was nothing left to say, anyway; it had already been said.

The silence grew. Finally Andrea turned toward the house. "I guess we'd better be getting back," she said. "We're going to have a busy day tomorrow."

Tony matched his stride to her slower pace as they directed their steps back toward the house. To their right, the bordering flowers stood beneath the moonlight. Tony wondered why they didn't seem as beautiful now as they had when he and Andrea had first started their walk.

Andrea looked across at him several times and wished he would turn and smile at her. But he didn't. He didn't hold her hand, either. It left her feeling very bereft.

Chapter Seven

Andrea woke very early the next morning. It was still dark and a glance at the digital clock beside her bed told her it was four fifty-five.

She climbed out of bed and put on a pink cotton robe. The house was quiet as she closed her bedroom door and made her way downstairs. Rosita and Luis wouldn't be up for another hour and a half, and Sara always slept late.

A light was on in the kitchen. Andrea pushed through the swinging doors, wondering if someone forgot to turn it off before bedtime.

"Oh! You're up."

Tony was at the sink fully dressed in boots, jeans and a pale yellow shirt. A glass coffeepot was in his hand. He turned at the sound of her voice and grinned to see the surprised look on her face.

"Did you think you had burglars?"

Smiling sleepily, she shook her head and walked on into the room. "No, I thought someone had left on the light. What are you doing up so early?"

He turned on the tap and thrust the glass carafe beneath the stream of cold water. "Making coffee. Where's Mama? Why doesn't she have breakfast cooked?"

Andrea laughed groggily and pushed the tousled hair out of her eyes. "Breakfast! Tony, it's only five o'clock. Rosita usually serves breakfast at seven."

He clucked his tongue and reached for the canister of coffee. "Andrea, you let her get by with murder. You're too softhearted."

"I happen to love your mother. And if I think she needs the extra rest now that she's gotten older, then I'm going to make sure she has it."

He chuckled. "You're the boss. I guess that's your prerogative."

She grabbed his hand as he started to dump the fifth spoonful of coffee grounds into the basket.

"It's my right to see that we have good coffee this morning. Give me that thing."

She gave him a little nudge and he stepped back to watch her finish making the coffee.

"Now you've hurt my feelings."

She tossed him a dry look. "Tony, I drank your coffee one time. I think I picked grains out of my teeth for two days afterward."

Andrea knew he was struggling to keep a straight face. "Okay, that did it," he told her. "I was going to cook your breakfast. But now I think you should cook mine to make up for that remark."

Andrea planted her hands on her hips and looked at him. She did her best to frown, but somehow her lips slanted into a soft melting smile. "If you cook like you make coffee, I think I'd better cook—to spare us both."

He grinned at her and thought how sexy and beautiful she looked with her hair tangled and her face bare of makeup. What would it be like to wake up every morning and find her beside him? Tony couldn't imagine anything that good.

"Can you actually cook?"

"Now what does that mean?" she retorted. Reaching inside the refrigerator, she pulled out eggs and bacon.

"It means just what I said. Can you cook?"

She gave him a haughty look. "Your mother has taught me how to cook several dishes."

"That doesn't tell me anything," he goaded.

"I can cook as well as I ride a horse. Does that answer your question?"

He pulled out a chair at the table and sat down to watch her work. The coffee was already starting to drip and the rich smell of it filled the room.

"Such conceit," he teased. "Where's that coming from?"

She threw him another dry look. "I don't know. There's something about you, Tony—it just seems to rub off."

He laughed and she smiled to herself. Last night she had slept deeply for the first time in a long time. She was certain it was because of Tony. His presence was putting everything back on kilter.

"Do you like running the ranch?" he asked suddenly.

Andrea carefully placed bacon slices on the griddle. "I *love* running the ranch. As you know, it's a hard job but a satisfying one. Naturally, I miss Dad. But I'm very determined to make this ranch go."

"You will. You're just stubborn and strong willed enough to make it work."

She turned away from her task long enough to glance at him. "Thank you, Tony, for believing in me. That means a lot."

Tony watched her as she broke eggs into a bowl and began to beat them with a wire whisk. Her soft curves were outlined by the thin fabric of the pink robe. Judging from the material and its simple lines, it wasn't an expensive garment. But her regal carriage made it seem that way.

His eyelids lowered as they feasted on the sight of her. He had the greatest urge to get up from the table and go to her. To slide his arms around her slim waist and draw her close to him. She would feel warm, and the faint sweet scent he'd always associated with her would drift up and fill his senses.

Tony had lain awake for a long time last night thinking about all she'd said to him. He knew she had been genuinely shocked to hear that her father had initiated his leaving. Apparently Roy Rawlins had never told her about that. On the other hand, was it possible that Andrea had really cared for him? To believe that she had felt something deeper for him caused his heart to swell with honor and something else he couldn't quite describe.

Even though his mind demanded that he stay put, he rose from the table and walked over to her.

Andrea glanced up and smiled at him as he sidled up to her. "I'm not giving you a choice about the eggs," she told him. "Scrambled is the easiest and quickest."

"I'll forgive you this time—if I find green chilies and onions in them."

Andrea picked up one of the green peppers she'd laid out with the rest of her ingredients. It pleased her to know she'd anticipated his taste. "You're a demanding man, Tony. Did you know that?"

He chuckled. "Zelda tells me that every day."

Thin rings of pepper began to fall from Andrea's paring knife. "I'll bet she doesn't know the half of it."

His closeness was a gift to treasure. She felt his warmth and breath and strength even though he wasn't touching her. She gave him a sidelong glance.

"How is it up there, Tony, living without any family around?"

He shrugged and she smiled inwardly, thinking no one could make the gesture as graceful as Tony. "I've become used to it. It gets lonely at times, but I've got a few friends around Albuquerque."

She wondered if those friends were women but restrained herself from asking. Last night she'd questioned him about a girlfriend and he'd danced around the answer. Maybe there *was* a special woman waiting for him back in Albuquerque. The idea was practically unbearable.

"Haven't you ever wanted to get married? Have a wife cooking breakfast for you instead of a housekeeper?" she asked, hoping her voice sounded light.

"I've known a few women. But none of them have inspired me to get married." He wondered why that was, and why having Andrea always by his side was such an appealing thought? He decided it was because she was different. Andrea had always been different from other women.

She reached out to turn the sizzling bacon. Tony watched her movements, felt her closeness and told himself that his first instinct about coming down here had been right. He was headed for trouble. He could sense disaster looming ahead of them and knew that somehow he had to stop it from striking. He just didn't know how.

After breakfast, Andrea suggested they go to the study where she could show Tony the ranch's business ledgers.

She refilled their coffee cups and carried them out of the kitchen and down the dark hallway.

Tony knew all about this house. Even though it had been years since he'd been inside it, he had quickly noted that very little had changed.

He walked ahead of Andrea so that he could open the door and switch on the light for her. One glance around told him that this long, wide room hadn't changed, either. Even the rose-beige carpet beneath his boots was just as he remembered.

Andrea carried the coffee to a massive oak desk situated at one end of the room. It faced a row of tall arched windows, which looked out over the back courtyard. At the moment the first pink streaks of dawn were beginning to light the sky.

Tony reached into his shirt pocket for a cigarette while Andrea took out the ledgers.

"No one ever worked on the books except for Dad, until he had the stroke," Andrea said. "And even then, it was a while before I knew about the money he had lost and the loans he'd taken out."

She pulled a straight-backed chair up next to the big leather one behind the desk. When she motioned for

Tony to take the big chair he said, "Andrea, there really isn't much need for me to look at the ledgers."

Andrea shook her head. "I know this has nothing to do with the loans. But I want you to look at the ledgers anyway. There may be something you'll see that could be trimmed away to save money. I'd be grateful for any advice. God knows, Dad never did teach me anything about business. I guess he figured he'd always be around."

Tony took the seat behind the desk and pulled the ledger up to him. At first glance he could only tell there had been endless transactions, but it did not take him long to see that the ranch needed all the help it could get.

When Tony finally leaned back in the chair and reached for his coffee cup, Andrea's blue eyes questioned him.

With a bleak grimace, he shoved the hair off his forehead. "Do you have a copy of the bank notes handy?"

Andrea left his side and crossed to a row of filing cabinets. A moment later she placed the yellow sheets of paper on the desk in front of him.

"You can imagine how I felt when I found them," she said grimly.

He lifted the papers and quickly scanned the figures and dates. Roy had always been his friend and he'd been good to Tony in many ways. But Tony believed at this moment he could have choked the older man for taking such unnecessary risks with his money. It had left a gigantic burden on Andrea—one that she certainly didn't deserve.

"I used part of Dad's life insurance to pay off the interest and defer the principal. This is what's due now."

Tony whistled under his breath. The numbers were staggering. "Andrea, this is incredible. From the looks of this, you're going to have to sell at least half the herd."

She let out a breath and sank down in the chair beside him. "I'd almost figured that. But cattle prices are fairly high now. That will help, won't it?"

"A little," he said thoughtfully, then reached again for the ledger. "As for trimming your working expenses, there are a few things here that sure need to be changed."

"Like what?" she asked, leaning closer to peer over his shoulder.

Tony's nostrils flared as her warm breath caressed his cheek. "This horse feed, for instance. You couldn't possibly need that much feed for the number of horses I saw last night."

"Larry changed brands, says this one is better. I know it's more expensive, especially since we pay for the feed company delivering it to the ranch."

"What do you mean, delivering it?" he echoed in disbelief.

She shrugged. "Just what I said. They haul it out to us. Larry says it's just as cheap to pay them as it is for him to drive into the city and haul it out himself."

Tony snorted. "Sounds like Larry likes to have his work done for him." He pointed to another figure on the ledger sheet. "And this vet bill, Andrea. It's outrageous."

"Yes, I thought so, too. But Larry doesn't know that much about doctoring animals and I felt it safer to call in a vet."

He looked at her impatiently. "Andrea, a foreman is supposed to know how to deal with the more common problems."

Her eyes met his. "I told you, he's not that experienced."

"You need a man who *is* experienced."

Andrea's tongue darted out to moisten her lips. She felt so breathless, so suddenly aware of the flame he sparked inside her.

"Men like you don't come along every day, Tony," she said, unaware that her voice had dropped to a shaky murmur.

One corner of his mouth lifted while a strange light flared in his eyes. "Are you trying to flatter me again, Andrea?"

She shook her head in answer.

"Then you want me to tell you I'll take over as foreman, is that it?"

Her lashes dipped, partially hiding the look in her blue eyes. "No, you're above that."

His eyes dropped to her moist lips. "Do you really believe that?"

"I've always believed it," she whispered with conviction.

It was impossible to keep her body motionless, to stop from leaning toward him.

"Andrea—this is—"

A knock at the doorway interrupted the moment. Andrea looked inquiringly over her shoulder to see Rosita. She wondered how much the older woman had witnessed.

"I found the mess in the kitchen. Why didn't you wake me?" She directed the question at Andrea.

Andrea smiled wryly and looked back at Tony. "I cook your breakfast and your mother calls it a mess. Can you beat that?"

Tony chuckled and glanced at his mother. "Andrea wanted to prove to me that she could cook as well as she rides a horse."

Rosita waved away his words. "You should have taken her out and let her ride the horse. Every pan in my kitchen is dirty! It's half your fault, Antonio!"

"Mine!" he burst out with feigned innocence. "Mama, I didn't—"

Ignoring his words, Rosita turned and left with a grumble. Andrea laughed and looked back at Tony.

"She thinks I'm messy. And she also considers the kitchen her private domain. I always have to *ask* her if I can cook something."

His eyes grew soft. "You really do love her, don't you?"

"Of course I love her," she answered. *And I love you, too, Tony,* she wanted to say.

Yet Andrea couldn't find a way to say the words. She was afraid that he wouldn't want to hear them or, even worse, that he would tell her he could never love her back.

Tony watched a troubled expression cross her face and wondered what she was thinking. They'd come so close to kissing. If his mother hadn't suddenly shown up, he couldn't have stopped it.

Sighing, Andrea rose from the chair and crossed to the arched windows. Dawn was breaking now. To the north, the desert mountains were awash with rose-gold sunlight.

"Morning has come," Tony said.

Andrea turned away from the window to find that he had followed her. "Mmm, it's beautiful, isn't it."

"Very beautiful," he agreed, then surprised her by reaching out and touching her hair.

His hand slid over its silky softness, then cupped the side of her face. Andrea wanted to rub her cheek against his rough palm.

"I know things must look very bleak to you, Andrea. But you'll overcome the loss. It will take a while, but sooner or later you'll get the cattle back."

He was doing his best to encourage her, to make her feel better, and that warmed her.

Andrea smiled up at him. "You're right. And I'm determined not to let any of it get me down."

His mouth took on a whimsical little twist and Andrea felt herself quiver as his thumb rubbed across her cheek.

"You know, it's really ironic to think that your father asked me to quit my job as foreman in order to separate us. Now, because of his bad investments, I'm back here on the Rio Vista and we're back together."

Back together. The words were so sweet, so precious. "I hope you don't regret it, Tony."

"Helping you? Never, Andrea." *But falling in love with you is another matter,* he thought. When this week was over, he'd have to return to Albuquerque and the Rocking R. He'd have to remind himself that he wasn't the sort of man she needed in her life. He wasn't the man she thought he was. He'd never get over it.

Andrea rose on her tiptoes and kissed his cheek. He smelled musky and masculine and the solid warmth of his body pulled at her. She didn't want to back away. She wanted to reach out and hold on to him.

Unwittingly he let his arms go around her, and for a moment Tony buried his face in her hair. But he knew a moment to touch her like this was all he could allow himself.

He stepped away from her, then reached out and touched her cheek. "I'd better be going. I told the men to be ready at seven so we could look the cattle over in the north pasture."

Andrea nodded, wondering if he could read the hazy love in her eyes. "I'll see you later."

His reply was a half grin and Andrea watched him walk to the door. Once he reached it he turned and gave her an impish wink.

"Don't tell Mama," he said, "but your breakfast was just as good as hers."

With that he disappeared down the hall. Andrea walked slowly over to the desk. The bank notes were still lying there as a solemn reminder. Somehow the sight of them didn't bother her as it would have before Tony came.

She gathered them and the ledgers and filed them away, then left the room.

Sara would be up by now. Andrea would get dressed and join her daughter at the breakfast table. Later, she'd get in one of the old work trucks and drive out to the north pasture to watch the men work. To watch Tony work.

A soft smile curved Andrea's lips as she climbed the staircase. She was behaving just as she had all those years ago when she'd been very young and Tony had made his home here on the ranch.

Her heart suddenly light, Andrea took the last few steps at a run.

Overhead, the sun was at its zenith. Its fierce heat glinted off metal and chrome as the pickup wound through the endless flat of choya and creosote bushes. Here and there spiny maguey and yucca shot tall and green above the desert floor. Red-brown dust billowed in the vehicle's wake. It spiraled up against the azure blue sky then sifted back to earth, settling on the yucca's white blossoms to turn them a coppery color.

The wind rushing through the cab was hot and dry, whipping Andrea's dark hair into a web of tangles. Across the seat Sara bounced and giggled with excitement.

The two of them were traveling through a rough-range section of the ranch. It had never been cleared or irrigated, yet it produced enough grama grass for grazing.

Yesterday, after she and Tony had looked over the ledgers, he had inspected as many cattle as time had allowed. Already he had made decisions on fifty head in the north pasture.

This morning Tony and the men had hauled out a truckload of portable panels. By this afternoon they hoped to have the fifty head rounded up, penned and loaded into stock trailers. Tomorrow they'd be prodded into a ring in the auction barn and sold to the highest bidder. Andrea would receive a check and one of the notes could be paid off.

It was a sad thought, but she refused to be depressed by it. Although she knew it was going to be a long tough road to restock them, she was thankful that at least she did have the cattle to sell.

Tony had said that she could save the ranch. Andrea was determined to live up to his opinion of her.

"I'm hungry, Mama. Can I have a sandwich?"

Andrea glanced down at her daughter. "We're almost there, Sara." Sulkily the little girl dropped her chin against her chest, and Andrea added, "Tony will want you to eat your sandwich with him. What will he think if you've already gobbled it down?"

Just the mention of Tony's name drew Sara to the edge of the seat, where the little girl peered earnestly over the dashboard. "Okay, Mama. But hurry!"

Andrea smiled faintly and reached over to pat the top of Sara's shiny head. It had only been three days since Tony had come to the ranch, yet already his presence had become very important to Sara. Whenever he was around, she vied for his attention. When he wasn't around, she wanted to go find him.

It was going to be very hard on Sara when Tony left to go home. But right now Andrea refused to even think of him going. It hurt too much.

Andrea geared down the truck as she came upon a rocky arroyo. Once she pulled up on the opposite side, they spotted the cattle. Dust clouded the air and hung over the maze of metal pens the men had erected.

As they drew closer, Sara began to shout and point to the far horizon. The men on horseback were slowly driving a small herd of cattle toward the portable corrals.

A safe distance away from the action, Andrea parked the pickup beneath a scraggly stand of mesquite trees.

Sara hurriedly climbed into the pickup bed to stand and watch the cowboys swinging their ropes after the straying cattle. Andrea lowered the truck's tailgate and hopped up on the edge to watch and wait.

Tony was easily recognizable in a copper-brown shirt and black hat. Andrea watched him work the dun-colored horse with the ease of a man long accustomed to a saddle. His lean body moved with the sudden bursts of power and abrupt cuts and turns of the horse as if he were part of it.

It was a joy to watch him. Smiling faintly, Andrea recalled how two or three of the hands had lost their seat riding the dun. She knew there wasn't any danger of it happening to Tony.

Five minutes later the cattle were safely penned and the men were tethering their horses. Tony was the first one to reach the truck.

He noticed one of Andrea's legs was curled beneath her while the other one swung gently back and forth over the edge of the tailgate.

For a moment he watched the toe of her boot slice the air with a lazy rhythm, then he allowed his gaze to slide up over her tight jeans and yellow shirt until finally he was looking into her eyes.

She smiled at him and said, "Hello."

They had talked at breakfast this morning before he'd left the house. But still she spoke to him as if each time they met was unique and special and needed to be treated that way. She'd always been like that in the past, and a warm pleasure stirred inside him at knowing she had not changed.

The curve of his mouth was unmistakably sensual as he smiled back at her. "Hello," he replied.

Andrea swung down from the tailgate and reached for the lid on the ice chest. Packed in the crushed ice were several cans of beer and a few soft drinks. She popped a lid on one of the beers and handed it to him. The cold foamy brew dripped down and over her fingers. She licked it off while Tony tilted back his head and took a long drink from the can.

"Looks like things are going smoothly. Have you had any trouble?" she asked.

He shook his head. "No trouble. How about you?"

She smiled ruefully. "The biggest part of my troubles is coming to a head, I think. Hopefully once these cattle are sold I can start looking at the bright side."

He nodded. "I was wondering, Andrea, if you'd thought about restocking the ranch with a less expensive breed. These are high-dollar cattle you've got right now."

"I'd been thinking about that, Tony. I was going to ask your opinion of the idea."

He pulled off his hat and swiped the dust and sweat from his forehead with his shirt sleeve. "You have a lot of land here, and to make it pay it's got to be used. I'd rather have fifty head of black baldys out there than fifteen or twenty purebreds."

Andrea was proud to find that she and Tony had similar thoughts on the subject of stock. If there was one thing she knew about him, it was that he was a smart rancher.

"I agree," she said as she watched him take another long swig of the cold beer. "Maybe you could come down and go to the auction with me when things get straightened out."

He lowered the beer can and Andrea could see the reservations on his face. Her spirits sank like a lead weight.

"I wouldn't count on it, Andrea," he said gently. "I can't just take off at a moment's notice."

"Oh, well, I could send up one of the men to watch over the Rocking R," she offered quickly.

Tony looked at her hopeful expression and wondered how he could possibly tell her that once he left, he'd never allow himself to see her again. "That'll be a long time from now, Andrea. By then you'll be trusting yourself to make these kinds of decisions."

In other words, once this week was over, that was it for him. He obviously didn't intend to ever come back. She suddenly had to look away from him to hide the mist in her eyes. "You're probably right, Tony," she said, her voice scratchy.

"Tony! Mama brought sandwiches," Sara announced as she hopped around the pickup bed. The heels of her cowboy boots made a clomping sound on the metal. Marveling at the racket, she stomped a bit harder, then giggled when her mother shot her a disapproving look.

"Sara, you're going to cause a stampede with all that noise," Andrea scolded lightly, but she was secretly glad for the disruption of her somber thoughts.

Sara's little face wrinkled with puzzlement. "What's a stampede?"

Chuckling, Tony reached for the girl and swung her up into his arms. "That's when a bunch of frightened animals take off in a run."

Sara giggled in a disbelieving way. "I couldn't do that. Once I tried to scare the bull through the gate and he wouldn't move."

"I hope you were on the outside of the fence," he told her.

Sara nodded. "I was, but when Mama wasn't looking I scratched him between the ears," she whispered conspiratorially.

Tony couldn't stop the smile on his face. "And what did the bull think of that?"

"Oh, he liked it! But Mama didn't when she caught me doing it!"

"I'll just bet your mama didn't like it," he agreed, while casting Andrea a wry grin.

"Are you ready to eat with us?" Sara asked him.

"I sure am," he told her. "Are you?"

"Yes!" She hugged his neck tightly and pressed her little cheek next to his. Sara's affection never failed to stir Tony. She looked up to him with all the adoration a child could give an adult. He knew he'd filled a void in her life, and he was beginning to realize the little girl was filling an empty place inside him that he hadn't even known was there.

He set her back down on the tailgate and swatted the bottom of her jeans. "Then help your mama so we can eat."

Just at that moment, Larry walked up behind them. Tony turned to see the foreman mopping the sweat from his face with a red bandana.

"Well, that's the last we'll be seein' of them," he said. "Personally, I think we'd be better off shipping out a bunch of those heifers."

Forgetting the basket of food for a moment, Andrea glanced up at the other man. "Why do you say that, Larry?"

"Why, these are good producers, Andrea. You know what you're gettin' with these. The heifers you never can tell. And you always lose a few of them anyway."

Andrea handed Tony a roast beef sandwich and caught his guarded gaze. She knew what he thought about Larry and none of it was good. She was beginning to agree with him.

"Andrea can hardly build a herd with only old cows," Tony replied.

Tony's manner was offhand but Andrea knew that underneath he was holding a rein on his temper.

"Damn," Larry spluttered. "These cows aren't old!"

"Most of them are."

At the sound of footsteps behind her, Andrea turned to see Pete and Windell had joined them. She was relieved at the interruption.

"Some of these cows back on this part of the ranch were here before I ever came along. And that's been a long time," Pete added. "Tony's right. If some of them need to be sold, these are the ones."

Larry squinted sullenly at Pete, opened his mouth to say something, then obviously decided against it.

Andrea went back to sorting out the sandwiches. It was obvious Larry didn't like Tony usurping his position or the other men siding with him, either. Something was going to have to be done about the foreman.

Once everyone had his food and drink, Andrea joined Tony and Sara. Tony was squatting on his boot heels at the base of a tree trunk while Sara sat at his right side. Andrea sank down on the ground next to her daughter, and Sara dimpled with enormous pleasure at being wedged between Tony and her mother.

"It's hot," Tony said to Andrea. "You should have sent Papa out with lunch."

Andrea shook her head and took a bite of her sandwich. "I wanted to see how things were coming along." She'd also wanted to see him. She wondered if he'd already guessed that.

Sara, too busy chewing, was unaware she was dropping part of her sandwich. Andrea reached over to help her, but Tony beat her to the task. Andrea settled back against the rough tree trunk and watched Tony straighten the sandwich and wipe a smear of mustard from Sara's cheek. He was always so kind and gentle with the child, and Andrea loved him for it.

"Mama, the cows are crying," Sara said.

Andrea looked out at the herd of cattle. Their restless movement had produced a rising cloud of dust up over the portable lots. "Yes, Sara. They're confused because they're boxed in."

Sara's little face wrinkled with concentration. "What will happen to them?"

Andrea sighed and did her best to push thoughts of Tony aside as she glanced down at her daughter. "They'll be sold and then they'll have a new home."

The child's blue eyes widened. "You mean they won't be hamburger meat?"

Shocked, Andrea lowered her sandwich and studied Sara intently. "Where did you hear such a thing?"

Sara ducked her head, knowing she'd been caught but unsure just how to get around it. "I—I snuck down to the horse stables and I heard Larry tell one of the other men."

Andrea lifted her head and looked across at Tony. His features were tight.

"What did Larry tell him?" Tony asked Sara in a low voice.

Deciding she wasn't in trouble for leaving the grounds around the house, Sara looked up at him eagerly. "He said that—" She glanced doubtfully over to her mother. "He said that Tony wanted to turn every cow on the ranch into hamburger meat. That isn't true, is it, Mama?''

Andrea was suddenly furiously angry, but she tried not to let it show in front of her daughter. "No! Of course not! Tony is here to help us.''

Sara smiled brightly, then snuggled her face next to Tony's arm. With sudden decision, Andrea started to rise to her feet. Tony's hand on her shoulder stopped her.

''Where are you going?''

She looked at him, surprised that he even had to ask. "You know where I'm going. I won't have him behaving this way.''

Tony shook his head. "Let it go for now.''

"Let it go! Tony, you're the one—''

Tony glanced down to see Sara watching them curiously. Reaching over Sara, he took hold of Andrea's arm and pulled her to her feet.

"Stay there and finish your sandwich,'' she told Sara.

They walked over to the pickup. Andrea stopped and stood with her back against the door. Tony propped one arm over her left shoulder. His body shielded her from the view of the others. She looked up at him with confusion. "Why not confront him? The way you've been talking I thought you'd like me to confront him.''

He shook his head. "I do believe Larry needs to be fired,'' he agreed. "But don't do it here where the other men will be a witness to it.''

"You think it would hurt the morale of the other men?'' she said.

One corner of his mouth lifted with dry humor. "In other words, it might scare the hell out of them.''

She let out a shaky chuckle. "Tony, what am I going to do once you're gone?" she asked in a half joking, half serious groan.

He was standing very close to her. With a will of their own, her fingers curled into his shirt where it opened at his throat. Tony's nostrils flared as his gaze rested on her mouth.

"I'll have to go, Andrea. I've told you that."

"I don't like to think so," she said.

"We don't always think the way we'd like to think, or do the things we'd like to do," he told her, then turned and walked back to where Sara sat beneath the mesquite tree.

He squatted down on his boot heels and Andrea looked at him, wondering if he'd been talking about her or himself.

Chapter Eight

Since another stock trailer was needed to haul the cattle, Tony drove back to the ranch with Andrea and Sara to fetch one.

As the pickup jostled over the rough, dusty terrain, Sara sat between the two adults and chattered constantly. By the time the ranch came into view, the child had managed to get both Tony and Andrea to agree to swim with her after supper.

Andrea had to admit she was looking forward to it. The last few weeks she hadn't taken much time off for relaxation of any sort, and having Tony with them would make it even nicer.

Tony drove the truck around to one of the barns. Parked beneath a deep overhanging shed was a white stock trailer. He backed the truck up to it and turned off the motor.

Andrea climbed to the ground, then held the door wide for Sara. The child took off in a run as soon as her feet hit the ground.

"Rosita's making cookies," Sara yelped happily, "and I'm gonna eat ten of them!"

"Sara," Andrea called after the girl, "not ten! And don't sneak back down here to the stables or you'll be in trouble."

Tony looked at Andrea and grinned. "Something tells me Sara gets into trouble quite often. Sort of like her mother used to."

Andrea wrinkled her nose at him. "She's inquisitive, nosy and stubborn. But she's also smart."

Tony chuckled. "She's very smart," he agreed, then asked, "Is my conceit rubbing off on you again?"

"Must be," she replied.

Tony noticed that the faint smile on her lips didn't match the troubled look in her eyes. She'd seemed unusually quiet on the drive back to the ranch. Putting his hand on her shoulder, he asked, "Are you worried about something, Andrea? Is firing Larry bothering you?"

It was dim and dusky beneath the tin shed after being out in the dazzling sunlight. Her blue eyes blinked before focusing on his face.

The concern in his expression pulled at something deep inside her. She wanted to reach out and take hold of him, to pour out what was really in her heart. But panic surged through her until all she could manage was a shake of her head.

"I know it's always hard to fire someone," he told her. "You feel guilty about taking their income. But in this case, Andrea, you must consider the ranch first."

"Yes, I know that, Tony," she sighed, then gave him a halfhearted smile. "I'm learning that being a boss hardens you in places."

His eyes lowered to the rounded swell of her breasts, then further to the slim circle of her waist. "You still look pretty soft to me," he said after lifting his gaze back to hers.

There was a teasing glint in his eyes, but there was something else there, too. Desire, maybe?

"Perhaps I should change my image," she said wryly. "I look soft and that's why Larry tried to take advantage of me."

His eyes suddenly narrowed to slits. "Andrea, are you saying—was he ever offensive to you?"

Andrea shook her head quickly to allay his suspicions. "No, he's never been suggestive in any way. I merely meant sloughing off his work."

Tony's rigid jaw relaxed somewhat. "If he had, I'd go beat the hell out of him right now!"

Andrea hated the idea of physical violence. But she had to admit it was nice to know Tony wanted to protect her, to defend her honor. In a way he'd always been Andrea's gallant knight. He still was, she supposed. A knight on a steed wearing a cowboy hat and boots instead of a suit of armor.

Her lips curved faintly at the idea. "Talk about *me* scaring the men, Tony. I wonder what that would do."

With an arrogant little chuckle, he turned and began to fit the trailer hitch over the ball on the truck bumper. "Don't worry, Andrea. I'll keep my left hook to myself."

He latched the safety chain then stood up and gave the hitch a testy kick with his boot. It stayed firm, and after tugging at the brim of his hat, he turned back to her.

"And don't worry about anything else. I like to see you smile, Andrea," he said, reaching out and touching the corner of her mouth.

Andrea breathed in deeply, smelling the pungent scent of the alfalfa hay stacked just behind them. She felt weak with heat even though there was a cool breeze blowing through the barn. "I'm not worrying, Tony," she spoke slowly. "I just keep thinking that in a few days you'll be leaving to—to go back to Albuquerque and—"

"Andrea," he quickly cut in, "I've already told you—"

"Yes, I know. You'll have to go back at the end of the week," she finished for him.

Her face had such a crushed look that he was hard put not to pull her into his arms. He wanted to kiss that look from her face. He wanted to see her eyes soft and drowsy with love for him. Damn it, Tony, you're asking to be hurt and you know it. Back away from her. Back away and save your heart.

"I know you've got a lot on your shoulders, Andrea. And I know you need someone to share the burden with. I know you need a foreman, but—"

She was suddenly exasperated with him for not knowing what she was trying to tell him, or for knowing and not wanting to acknowledge it. "Yes, I do need all those things, Tony. But that's not why I want you to stay—I—it's been so good having you back. I—"

His black brows drew together in a frown and Andrea's lips clamped shut then opened to snap, "Tony, I used to think you were one of the most romantic men

I'd ever known. But now—I—oh, forget it," she muttered.

Turning on her heel, she fled from the barn. She was both hurt and embarrassed and doing her best to hide it behind a mask of anger.

"Andrea, come back here!"

Halting her steps, she looked back over her shoulder at him. "Go on to the men and the cattle, Tony! You don't want to hear what I have to say, anyway!"

"Andrea—"

For a moment he looked as if he might come after her. Andrea didn't give him the chance. She took off in a run toward the house.

She was more than halfway there when she realized there were tears on her cheeks.

It was time for supper. Andrea had just changed into a cotton dress with a scoop neckline and a full skirt. It was pale pink and the soft material swished against her bare calves as she walked to the dressing table and picked up her hairbrush.

A knock at the door halted her rhythmic strokes. Laying the brush aside, Andrea crossed the bedroom to open the door.

To her surprise, Tony was standing in the hallway, dressed in fresh jeans and a white shirt with a bunch of desert flowers clutched in his hand. His face was dark and very serious.

"Don't ever say I'm not romantic, Andrea. That's not the thing to say to a Mexican."

Andrea had the urge to burst into both giggles and tears. "I take it those are for me?"

He flashed her a charming smile. "No one else," he drawled. "Are you ready to go down to supper? I'll have Mama put these in something for you."

She nodded and stepped out into the hall to join him. "Here, let me carry those." She took the flowers from him and lifted them to her face. They had a tangy wild smell that Andrea loved because it reminded her of the desert.

Lifting her eyes to him, she said, "Thank you, Tony. You're so—"

"Romantic," he finished for her, his smile growing a bit devilish. "Come on, you can say it, Andrea. I'm romantic."

"Okay, Tony. You are romantic. I'll never doubt you again."

The lines around his mouth deepened and he held his arm out to her. Andrea curved her fingers around it and they started down the stairway.

"That's good, Andrea. You shouldn't doubt me." He cut her a sidelong glance that was both sexy and sweet. "Will you smile for me now?"

Andrea knew that no matter what, she could never stay angry or hurt when Tony was around. And even though her heart was aching at the thought of him leaving, she would smile for him anyway, because she loved him. "Yes, I will smile for you, Tony."

Supper that night was one of the biggest Rosita had prepared so far. She'd made smoked ribs and smothered them with hot Texas-style barbecue sauce. They had to be eaten with your fingers and they were sinfully rich and messy, but oh so delicious. Everyone's plate was piled with bones when the meal was over.

Afterward, Andrea helped Rosita clean up the mess while Tony went with his father to the barn to finish a chore Luis had started earlier in the day.

It was growing dark when the two men returned. Andrea was relaxing in a lounge chair on the patio while Sara sat impatiently at her mother's side and attempted to read a storybook.

"Tony, are you ready to swim?" Sara asked, jumping to her feet when he appeared out on the patio.

"If you ladies are."

Sara looked eagerly over to her mother. "Are you ready now, Mama? Come on, let's get our suits on!"

Andrea pushed herself up from the chair and gave Tony a wry grin. "Ready to get wet?"

"Do I hear a little mischief in your voice, Andrea?"

She merely answered him with a chuckle and reached for Sara's hand. "We'll be back shortly," she told him.

Tony was sitting on the diving board dressed in a pair of faded cutoff jeans when they returned to the patio. Andrea tried not to stare at the dark beauty of his muscular body. It was very hard to keep her eyes from him when all sorts of erotic thoughts were dancing through her head.

Sara, wearing a red-and-white ruffled bikini, ran out on the long board to join him. "Look at me, Tony! Do I look pretty?"

She jumped on her toes beside him, making both of them bounce on the swaying board. "You look just like a movie star," he told her, his eyes filled with indulgence for her.

"Tony," she giggled. "You're joshin' me."

"I don't josh pretty girls," he insisted with a dazzling white grin. "And you know what else? I've decided no one can get in the pool unless they dive in."

"Yeah! Yeah!" Sara squealed in delighted agreement.

"Tony—" Andrea began in a guarded tone.

Ignoring the beginning of Andrea's protest, he said to Sara, "You can go first to show me and your mama the best way to do it."

Andrea peeled off her white cover-up and slowly joined them on the board. "Tony, who appointed you the boss around here?" she asked teasingly.

He turned his head to see her standing a few feet away. "You did, remember?"

His hazel eyes narrowed at the sight of her. The white swimming suit she wore was cut skimpily out of a puckery fabric that clung to her curves. She looked like a delicious toasted marshmallow. All white and brown, soft and sweet.

She smiled and sat down beside him. The board was still warm from the hot afternoon sun. It felt good. So did looking at Tony.

"I suppose I did, didn't I." She sighed dramatically. "But since you know I'm scared to death of diving, you're going to let me jump in."

He slanted her a provocative look that had Andrea's heart thudding with warm desire. "We'll see."

"Are you ready to watch me?" Sara chimed out.

The child's voice broke the glance between them. Andrea looked up at her daughter. "Yes, darling. Go ahead and show us one of your very best dives."

Tony and Andrea scooted back toward the edge of the pool and let Sara have the end of the diving board. After an exaggerated show of preparation, Sara jumped into the air, then entered the water with a smooth clean dive.

When her little head broke the surface of the water, Tony and Andrea gave her a loud round of applause.

"That was great, Sara," Tony exclaimed. "Now watch your mama and me. We're going to make a great entrance and dive in together."

Tony took hold of Andrea's hand and pulled her to her feet. She cocked her head to one side as she studied him with a guarded expression.

"Tony, this had better be very simple," she warned.

"My little chicken," he soothed, "you know I wouldn't do anything to hurt you."

Tony knew she had an unusual fear about diving, even though she could swim like a fish. He and his brothers had sometimes come up to the big house and used the pool with her. Tony had urged, cajoled, pleaded, done everything he could to help her get over her fear, but nothing had worked.

"I don't want to dive, Tony," she said, feeling the old panic rise up in her. "Let's just jump."

He shook his head. "That wouldn't be fair to Sara."

"That's right, Mama. You have to dive. You can do it!" Sara joined in.

Andrea gripped his hand a bit tighter. "Tony, no. I don't want to."

His eyes took on a sudden gleam and she knew if she didn't do something he was going to dive in and pull her along with him. In a sudden panic she tried to jerk away from him.

Tony tightened his hold and said in a soft calming voice, "Andrea, don't be frightened. I'll be right here beside you."

"No—no!"

She reached out in an attempt to push him away, but he merely captured her free hand and held her steady. "Andrea, I thought you trusted me."

Andrea cast him a hesitant glance. "I—I do."

"Then you know that I won't let anything happen to you, don't you?"

His expression was sincere, so serious that it calmed her. She took a deep breath and nodded stiffly. "I know you won't."

"Then there's nothing to be frightened of. We're going to take one bounce, then go, okay?"

She wanted to say yes, but the water looked so far below them. To imagine going face forward into it practically paralyzed her. "I—you won't let go of me, will you?"

"I'll have a hold on you the whole time. I won't let go," he assured her in a soft gentle voice. "We'll be together all the way."

Something about those last words soothed her somewhat. "Okay, let's go before I back out."

His grin was dazzling and filled with triumphant pleasure. The last thing that ran through Andrea's mind as they hit the water was that smile and the fact that Tony was still holding on to her hand just as he'd promised.

Their heads broke the surface of the water at the same time. Andrea was coughing and spluttering.

"Are you all right, Andrea?" he asked anxiously, curling one arm around her waist and treading water for both of them.

Once Andrea caught her breath, she laughed with glee and flung her arms around his neck, taking Tony by surprise. "I did it, Tony! I really did it!"

He laughed with pleasure. "Yes, you really did it. It wasn't all that bad now, was it?"

"It was great fun! Shall we do it again?"

And so the next hour went by as the three of them played and laughed in the pool.

Sara was one tired little girl when Rosita took her into the house for cookies and milk, then bed.

Andrea sat by the side of the pool, letting the warm night wind dry her hair. Tony had gone to fetch his cigarettes and she looked up as he suddenly reappeared by her side.

"Did Rosita give you cookies and milk, too?" she asked, her cheeks dimpling up at him.

He shook his head and eased down beside her. "I'm still full from dinner. How about you?"

"I didn't eat as much as you did," she said.

He looked at her and chuckled as he put a cigarette between his lips. "But you ate enough of that chocolate cake to kill a horse."

Andrea watched his dark lean fingers take a match from the small box and strike it against the side. His movements were easy, economical and very masculine. She'd always thought he had sexy hands, but now as she looked at them she saw that and so much more. Skill, strength, tenderness, protectiveness. Earlier, when they'd made the dive, she'd held on to his hand and had been unafraid. She realized it was love that chased away her fear.

"I haven't lost my sweet tooth," she explained. "Especially for chocolate."

He exhaled the cigarette smoke and said, "I remember when you used to ride out to where I was working and you'd always have a snack for me tied on to your saddle. I'd hope you would bring ham or a piece of cheese or a chicken leg. But it was always candy bars or chocolate kisses.''

Andrea chuckled and leaned back on the thick towel. Propping up the side of her face with one hand, she looked at him and smiled in the darkness. "That's because I wanted you to have the sugar for energy."

"Hmmph. That's because you wanted to help me eat them."

She laughed. It was true and Tony had known it. Shifting, she lay on her back and looked up at the sky. It seemed very close tonight.

"Thank you, Tony."

"For what?" he murmured, his back still turned to her as he finished his cigarette.

"For making me dive and helping me not to be afraid."

"I wasn't really going to force you. You faced your fear all by yourself."

Her eyes dropped from the starry sky to his broad back. Lean muscle rippled beneath his brown skin as he leaned over to stub out his cigarette.

"I dived because you were beside me, Tony. And you know that."

He didn't say anything and Andrea realized that it had always been like this. Tony made her see problems and fears in a rational way. He made it easy for her to face them. The problems with the ranch were the biggest she'd ever come up against, but so far she hadn't panicked, she hadn't fallen apart. She was positive she could overcome them now, and all because Tony had said she could.

He wouldn't be holding her hand along the way. He would be gone. But still she would hold him in her heart and hope that it would be enough to get her through.

"I don't suppose you had a chance to talk to Larry?" he asked.

He glanced back over his shoulder at her and Andrea shook her head.

"After the men headed to the stockyards with the cattle, I didn't see him anywhere," she told him.

"Would you like for me to break the news to him?"

"That would be pushing a dirty job on you," she said. She certainly didn't want Tony to think she was using him.

"I can handle dirty jobs. Besides, it will probably be a lot easier for him to take, coming from a man instead of a woman."

"I hadn't thought of it that way," she admitted.

"I've been thinking that Windell would make a good foreman."

His statement surprised her. She sat up and looked across the few inches between them at his face.

"Windell? He's so bashful. How could he ever give out orders? And he's so young."

"I wasn't much older than that when your papa made me the foreman," he reasoned.

"That's true, but you were different."

He turned full face to look at her. "How?"

"I don't know. You were just—more weathered."

His mouth crooked upward. "You mean I'd already had to learn to be a scrapper in order to survive? Well, just be glad Windell had it better. I am."

"I don't think anyone should have to go through a poor tough background just to gain experience," she told him. "All I'm trying to say is that Windell doesn't know as much about cattle or ranching as you did at that age. He doesn't even know as much as Larry, and that's precious little."

Tony shrugged. "He'll learn. Just like I did. He's got motivation and that's what it really takes."

"Tony," she softly accused, "you've got a soft spot. Did you know that?"

"No, I don't," he countered, but she could see a glimpse of his white teeth as he tried not to smile at her. "I'm a man of steel."

She reached out and touched his shoulder, then let her fingers slide down and smooth across his collarbone. "You don't feel like steel to me," she murmured.

Andrea heard his breath draw in ever so slightly. "Andrea, are you trying to seduce me?"

Her hand slid further over the thick muscle of his chest. Flattening her palm against it, she rubbed gently back and forth.

"Maybe I am," she whispered.

She shifted and closed the gap between their faces. The warmth and smell of him, the touch of him stirred her as nothing else ever had. Desire was pulsing warm inside her. Her breasts felt heavy and tingly and she knew her nipples were hard and straining against the fabric of her swimsuit. She wanted him, loved him. It was all so pure and simple for her. Why couldn't it be that way for him?

"You're either afraid to kiss me, or you just don't want to," she told him.

Tony watched the movement of her lips and felt everything within him burgeon and tighten. She was like no other woman to him and he suddenly knew why. He loved her. The realization stabbed at him. He felt his throat thicken, his hands quiver, as he reached for her.

"My Andrea."

It was all he could say before his mouth closed over hers.

Days had passed since he'd kissed her on the Rocking R. She'd hungered for him all that time and now she feasted on his lips, let her hands and fingers reacquaint themselves with the feel of his hair, his skin, the curve of his face.

Her urgency fueled the yearning inside him. With a soft growl, Tony lowered her down on the damp towel spread across the tile.

Andrea shifted beneath him and marveled at how perfect it felt to be next to him, to wind her bare legs through his and press herself close.

When his lips finally released hers to slide against her throat, she could not stop the words inside her from bursting forth.

"Oh, Tony, don't you know by now that I love you?"

Her words had a sobering effect. She could feel him stiffen against her long before he lifted his head and looked in her eyes.

"No."

Andrea realized he'd whispered the denial more to himself than to her. She caught his face between her palms.

"I've tried to tell you in so many ways."

He eased away from her, and she looked up at his dark brooding face.

"You've told me that you want me to stay. That's all."

"Tony," she began, while quickly scrambling to a sitting position. "I don't think you understand."

The pained confusion on her face had him rising to his feet and reaching for his cigarettes. Turning his back to her, he fumbled with the matchbox, then with a muttered curse crushed it in his fist.

"I do understand," he said in a low raspy voice. "I understand that as of tomorrow you'll be without a foreman. You need someone to help you pull this place together. Saying 'I love you, Tony,' would solve both problems."

The words slashed deep, stunning her with pain and disbelief. Slowly her fingers lifted to her mouth, then her head swung jerkily back and forth.

"You can't mean that," she whispered hoarsely.

"Why not? I haven't seen you in six years. Then you suddenly show up on my front door asking me for help. Now, a few days later, on the very day you decide to fire your foreman, you tell me you love me. What does that sound like to you?"

"It sounds like I'm talking to an ass instead of Tony Ramirez!" she shot back with sudden fury. "Have you forgotten that you're the one who advised me to fire Larry?"

She could see his teeth were grinding together in anger. Andrea had never had the urge to slap anyone until now.

"I think you knew Larry was going to have to be fired long before you ever came to me in Albuquerque," he ground out.

Had she? Maybe, but that had absolutely nothing to do with the way she felt about Tony. She had to make him realize this. "Maybe I was considering it then. But that has nothing to do with—with what I feel for you."

His stare was hard and unbending. "Six years ago I was good enough to run your papa's ranch but not good enough to marry his daughter. I'm still that same man, Andrea. So why should I believe anything is different now?"

Tears were suddenly burning her throat and eyes. "That's totally unfair, Tony."

He looked away from her. "It was unfair for you to ask me to come here. I wish to hell you'd never come to Albuquerque!"

Andrea couldn't bear any more. She snatched up her cotton cover-up and scrambled to her feet. "I always seem to make the mistake of thinking you might care about me. You just made sure, Tony, that I will never make that mistake again."

Without waiting for his reply, Andrea ran across the patio and into the house. Thankfully it was quiet and dark. She hurried up the stairs and down to her bedroom. Once inside she locked the door behind her, then slumped weakly down on the dressing bench at the end of the bed.

Hot tears scorched her cheeks and her shoulders shook as she sat there weeping in the darkness. Love was supposed to be wonderful, beautiful. So why was her heart aching as it had never ached before?

"Andrea, let me in." The words were followed by a twist of the doorknob.

Startled, Andrea lifted her head and stared at the door. "You've already said all you needed to, Tony."

"Andrea," he muttered. "Open the door."

"No."

She heard him moving away from the door. But not until she was certain he was gone did she allow herself a deep breath. Yet no sooner had Andrea exhaled than a footstep sounded out on the balcony. With a sudden jerk, she turned toward the sliding glass door that separated her bedroom from the outside. Tony was there, already pushing it aside.

Rising to her feet, she said, "What is it, Tony? Have you come to tell me that I'd better keep everything on a business level? You wasted your time—you already got that point across. And you can stop worrying that I asked you down here to beguile you or take advantage of you. I'll have a check made out for you when you get ready to leave. It will be as fair as I can make it."

He stepped inside the room but did not slide shut the glass door behind him. Andrea felt naked in more ways than one as she stood there in her bathing suit, trembling beneath his dark gaze.

"I don't want your money," he said quietly.

She hugged her arms around her waist as her lips twisted ruefully. "You don't want my money, my affection or my love. I guess that covers about everything, Tony," she said in a dry painful tone.

He stepped closer until there were only inches separating them. His eyes on her face, he said, "I didn't mean that, Andrea, about wishing you'd never come to Albuquerque."

The short laugh that slipped past her lips was brittle. "I think you did. But that doesn't matter. This whole thing was my fault. It was foolish of me to think that just because I love you it would mean anything to you—that you would return it."

"Andrea—"

"No," she interrupted, quickly stepping around him. "I realize I was expecting too much from you."

He watched her walk out on the balcony, her body stiff, her head high. She looked like a goddess to him and for a moment he wanted to forget everything and carry her back to the bed and make love to her in the soft darkness, away from the outside world.

God help him, he didn't know anymore what was right—or for the best—for either of them.

"Andrea, didn't you hear me down there a moment ago? I'm still that same poor Mexican. You don't love me. And even if you did, it would never work for us."

He'd come up behind her and now she whirled around to look at him. Her eyes were searching and pleading. "Why? Why wouldn't it?"

Tony took her by the shoulders and turned her so that she was facing the railing of the balcony. He pointed toward the southwest where the border cities lay twinkling in the darkness.

"Because there is a border between us, Andrea. Just like the Rio Grande that cuts through the desert and separates these two cities. I'm on one side. You're on the other."

Her head swung slowly back and forth. "Borders can be crossed."

His fingers gently pressed into her skin. "I've seen them wade across, thinking, hoping they are headed for a better life. But it hardly ever works out that way. They are usually caught and taken back by the Border Patrol, and even if they aren't caught they wind up going back on their own because they can't fit into a world so different from theirs."

She looked up to meet his gaze. "You're a U.S. citizen. None of that applies to you."

"I'm merely trying to tell you that there's a wide gap between us. We'd be asking for trouble and heartache to try to bridge it. You don't need that and neither do I."

He obviously didn't think loving her was worth the risk. Loving her. Damn it, Andrea, why don't you face it? That's the whole problem. The man just doesn't love you.

She pushed away from him and the railing. "It's getting late. I'm going to bed," she said with sudden decision.

"Andrea—"

Resting her hand on the glass door, she turned to look back at him.

He took a step toward her then stopped. "Deep down, I didn't really think you were using me. It's just that—it's hard for me to think that a woman like you could care for me. I mean really care for me." He shook his head and thrust one hand through his tousled hair. "I don't want you to remember me that way."

She swallowed painfully. "What way?"

"Being defensive, accusing you of things you don't understand. Hurting you. That's not really me."

Fresh tears burned her eyes. She hoped he couldn't see them. "I know it's not, Tony. And it's all right. I'll see you tomorrow."

And the day after that, I'll tell you goodbye, her heart added. She slipped inside the room and didn't watch him walk away.

Chapter Nine

J ennifer's mother is going to pick me up at nine o'clock.'' Sara spoke with great importance. "And we're going shopping and then we're going to the park for a picnic."

Andrea glanced across the breakfast table at her daughter, who was busily narrating the day's upcoming events for Tony. He was giving her his undivided attention while Rosita ladled eggs onto his plate.

"That sounds like lots of fun," Tony agreed.

"Will you be here to meet my friend?" Sara asked.

Tony glanced across the table at Andrea, then back at the child. "I'm afraid not, Sara. Your mama and I are going to the stockyards this morning. Maybe I can see your friend another time before I go home."

Sara looked thoroughly disappointed, making Andrea wonder if it was because Tony wasn't going to be here to meet Jennifer or simply because he was leaving.

Andrea smiled gently and reached to pat her daughter's cheek. "You'd better eat so that you'll be ready when Jennifer gets here," she urged.

"You won't be gone when I get back, will you?" Sara asked him in a pathetic little voice.

Tony gave her a reassuring smile. "You know I wouldn't leave without telling my best girl goodbye."

Pacified for the moment, Sara gave him a big grin and dug into the eggs on her plate. Across the table, Andrea felt her heart crack a little more.

Rosita got the coffeepot and refilled her cup and Tony's. The older woman glanced curiously from Andrea to Tony and back to Andrea again. Andrea figured Rosita had probably noticed how unusually quiet they both were this morning. From the scowl on Rosita's face, she knew Tony's mother didn't like this turn of events. But then neither did Andrea.

She looked across the table at him and thought that his eyes looked tired, as if he hadn't slept. Andrea could have told him she had slept very little herself. She had lain there for hours thinking about him being in the room next to her and how she longed to go to him.

Yet Andrea had not gone to him. He'd made things clear to her last night. He didn't want to hurt her. And he didn't want to love her. Hurt and love. Love and hurt. Would she ever be able to separate the two?

Tony glanced up suddenly and caught her looking at him, but he didn't smile at her as he normally would have.

"Can you be ready in an hour?"

She gave him a short nod. "I'll meet you out back by the garage."

After breakfast, Andrea went upstairs with Sara to help the child pack the things she was taking with her for today's outing with Jennifer.

Once Sara was dressed and ready, Andrea sent her downstairs to wait for her company. Andrea went to her own bedroom and quickly showered.

Dried and dusted with talc, she pulled on a pair of black jeans and boots and a mauve-colored shirt. She was sitting at her dressing table applying makeup when Rosita stuck her head around the bedroom door.

"*Niña*, Tony says to tell you he's ready."

"Thank you, Rosita. I'll be right down."

Rosita's lips thinned as she watched Andrea smooth blush on her cheeks. "What happened between you and Tony last night? I've never seen either one of you looking so unhappy."

Andrea kept her gaze carefully on her own image instead of turning to Rosita. "That's probably because we both are," she answered simply.

Rosita snorted impatiently. "You've been happier since Tony's been here than I've seen you in years. And Tony cares about you. I can read it all over him."

Andrea's head dropped sadly. "Tony is leaving tomorrow morning. That proves how much he cares."

"You've got to persuade him to stay, Andrea. You and Tony belong together. Either here or in Albuquerque, I don't care where. I just believe you were meant for each other."

Tears burned Andrea's eyes. "I do, too," she whispered hoarsely. "But Tony has other ideas."

Rosita gave her a hard, meaningful look. "Tony has a lot of pride, especially where you are concerned. It's gonna be up to you to make him see things clearly."

Andrea groaned to herself as Rosita whirled and left the doorway. Did the woman think changing her son's mind would be that simple?

Rising to her feet, she gave her image one last critical look, then turned to leave the room. She was about to go out the door when a sudden thought made her retrace her steps.

Back at her dressing table, she reached for her jewelry box and pulled out the silver bracelet Tony had given her so long ago. Would he notice it? Would he even remember giving it to her? she wondered. Andrea quickly fastened it around her wrist and left the room.

Tony was backing the small sports car out of the garage as she crossed the back patio.

"I was beginning to wonder what was keeping you," he said, holding the car door open for her.

Andrea smiled faintly as she slid onto the seat. "I'm just running late. Sara had a hard time deciding what she wanted to wear."

Tony sat behind the wheel and started the car toward the graveled drive. "They always auction the hogs before the cattle anyway. We have plenty of time."

She nodded as the car passed the house and they started toward the main highway. From the corner of her eye she took in the sight of him in his mustard-colored shirt, black jeans, hat and boots. The dark color suited his tough masculinity and Andrea knew that today women would look at him and think him handsome.

"You are officially without a foreman now," he suddenly informed her. "Larry left a few minutes ago with a few choice words and the wages you owed him.''

Andrea grimaced. ''I'm sorry about that. But you were right—I have to consider the ranch first.''

Tony looked across at her as he guided the car past the bright cannas that bordered the drive stretching across Rio Vista land.

Last night he'd told her that he didn't believe her feelings for him were connected to the ranch. But now in the light of day, he wondered. Andrea had been under a lot of pressure, and Tony had come along at a time when she needed someone. Was she desperate and he merely convenient?

Damn it, Tony, don't keep thinking about it! It's just like you told her anyway. There was a border between them and it was a long way across it.

''You look very pretty this morning.''

She glanced at him, then down at her hands lying loose in her lap. There was a pain in her breast as she took a deep breath. ''Thank you, Tony.''

''The weather is perfect this morning. There should be a big turnout of buyers at the stockyards.''

Andrea glanced out the car window to see that the morning was indeed beautiful, with only an occasional cloud floating here and there across the azure sky. El Paso was beautiful at any time but Andrea especially loved summer, the hot days and warm nights.

She wondered how Albuquerque would be in summertime, then told her heart to forget it. Tony had made it clear that he wasn't interested. She'd never see either the Rocking R or Tony again.

The stockyards were enormous. She and Tony were forced to park a far distance from the sale barn. The two of them walked along the edge of the stock pens and dodged in and out of the people milling to and from the building.

Dust and the smell of livestock filled the air. The chaotic sound of bawling cattle competed with that of the auctioneer's amplified voice. Pickups and stock trailers were parked everywhere, and at one of the loading docks a semitrailer was unloading several head of Mexican steers.

"At least the market isn't flooded at this time of year," she said as both of them looked out over the maze of penned cattle.

"That's true. The prices should hold pretty steady," he said, then put his hand on her arm and halted her steps. "This isn't going to get you down, is it? I mean seeing the cattle go?"

His hazel eyes were filled with concern. As Rosita said, he did care for her. She had seen that the past few days. But caring wasn't loving. Forcing a bright smile on her face, she said, "No, it won't bother me. I'll just be glad to get all this straightened out."

Seemingly satisfied by her answer, Tony released her arm, and they continued to walk on toward the barn.

After a moment Tony said, "I'm going to take Windell aside this afternoon and point out the other cattle that will have to go. The men can tag them and have them ready by next week. I won't be here, but the men will know what to do. I'd suggest you lot feed them a couple of days before hauling them to sale. I know that might sound expensive, but they'll weigh out much better if you do."

She nodded, understanding and agreeing with everything he said. "Yes, I'll make sure the men do that."

"If the cattle don't bring enough to cover the notes, I think you should consider selling three or four of the horses. Since you don't have as many cattle to work now, you won't be needing them anyway."

As they entered the dim interior of the building, Andrea said, "And they don't produce like a cow. Which ones do you think should be sold?"

Putting his hand at the small of her back, Tony guided her up the steps of bleachers. "I'll discuss it with Windell. We'll pick them out this evening."

So everything will be taken care of when he leaves, Andrea thought glumly as they took a seat in one of the empty spaces on the bleachers. Well, she'd asked for one week and that was what he'd given her. He'd done everything he'd promised. It wasn't his fault Andrea wanted more of him. But she couldn't help it. She loved him, and thinking of him leaving was tearing at her heart.

A big crowd was gathered on the seats circling the show pen. Andrea glanced around her at the sea of cowboy hats. Some were straw, others felt. Some of the men were old, others young. Cattle was still primarily a man's business. But there were women here, too. Yet she figured most of them were wives enjoying a day at the sale with their husbands.

The thought made her feel very lonely and a bit vulnerable, but Andrea tried to keep her expression from revealing how she felt.

Presently there were hogs in the pen. Andrea had never been able to keep up with the auctioneer's voice. She leaned over close to Tony's ear and asked, "What are they going for?"

"Today you can buy a hog weighing two and a quarter for a little over a hundred dollars," he said, then grinned at her rather impishly. "Why? Thinking about going into the hog business?"

She shook her head and felt her spirits lift a bit at the sight of his smile.

"No," she said. "I was merely checking to see if you really knew what he was saying."

He gave her a dry look. "You can't understand him?"

"No! How can anyone understand that mumbling jabber? I could never understand it, even when I came here with Dad. So what is he saying now?"

"He's saying forty-six thirty a hundred. No, someone just bid. Now it's gone to forty-six fifty."

Andrea listened intently but couldn't make out any of the numbers or words. "I can't understand any of that."

God, what was she going to do when it did come time for her to buy stocker cattle? She wouldn't know what she was paying for them, when to bid, when to stop, how much she should even give, he thought grimly.

She had asked Tony if he would come down and help her when that time came. And he'd told her that he couldn't. He had to stick with that decision. She wasn't his responsibility. He'd helped her this week. But now it had to stop. It all had to stop!

"You'll have to hire a buyer when you go to restock," he said.

She shot him an indignant look. "I will not pay some man a percentage just to sit there and bid for me! I'll learn how to do it if I have to come down here every day."

Like hell, he thought. Sitting alone among all these cowboys, she'd be like a steak to a pack of hungry hounds.

"That wouldn't be very reasonable, Andrea."

Andrea's brows inched up. "Reasonable?" she repeated while trying to read the impassive smoothness of his face. "That's not important right now. My top priority is to be economical in every way I can be."

"You can't be economical if you don't know what you're doing." It was the wrong thing to say to her; he knew it as soon as the words were out and her eyes sparked with determination.

"Tony, I'm not stupid. I can learn. I know what kind of cattle I want. I'll study the market prices, and if need be I'll bring one of the men down here with me. Surely one of them can understand this auctioneer jargon."

He didn't want another man down here with her. Didn't she know that? He loved her. He should be the one by her side, guiding her, helping her, protecting her, sharing her life.

Damn it, Tony, she deserves more than you. You've got to forget how you feel about her, put it out of your mind and get back to Albuquerque. She'll find someone then, someone who can give her much more than you can.

His eyes were drawn to her lips and he wondered how soon it would be before some other man kissed them. Last night they had felt like rich velvet beneath his mouth and she'd kissed him with warmth and passion. He wanted to think that he was the only man she could kiss that way; the only man she would want to kiss.

Andrea watched his jaw grow tighter and tighter. Obviously he disapproved of her idea. "Tony, I know that in the past Dad always protected and pampered me. But I'm not lazy. You know that I've never been afraid of work or getting my hands dirty. I can do this. I can do anything it takes to keep the ranch going. Even if that means shoveling horse manure out of the stables."

Her lips were moving and Tony knew she was speaking but it was a struggle to shake off his thoughts and lift his eyes to hers.

"I'd better not hear of you doing stable work, Andrea. You weren't meant for that sort of thing."

She laughed softly. "Tony, I wasn't born on a pedestal. Why do you keep trying to put me on one?"

Because she was soft and precious, beautiful and loving. Maybe it was his Latin blood, or maybe it was just the way he thought that made him react this way. Or maybe it was the fact that he loved her. Whatever the reason, he could not change his feelings.

He reached over and took her hands in his. They were small and soft. To touch them and hold them made him feel like a man. A man who wanted to love and protect her.

"These hands were not made for handling a rake and shovel," he said.

A new herd of hogs squealed in protest as a barn worker prodded them into the show ring. However, Andrea didn't notice the smell or the sound of them. She was too caught up in Tony's touch, the strange look in his eyes.

"Oh?" she asked with a wry smile. "What were they made for, Tony?"

These soft little hands could soothe and calm him, he thought, or wring a heated desire from deep inside him. To Tony, they were magic, and in spite of their surroundings, he wanted to lift her fingers to his lips.

Andrea watched his eyes drop to their clasped hands. It was then that he noticed the bracelet and her heart went still as he fingered the small disk.

"You kept this during all these years."

His eyes and his voice were filled with a mixture of wonder and pain as though he couldn't quite believe, or didn't want to believe, that he or the bracelet could mean so much to her.

"Yes," she said. "I have everything you've ever given me."

The bits of ribbon for her hair, the little stuffed bear, the tin heart filled with chocolates. They were all precious to her simply because Tony had given them to her.

His mouth twisted ruefully as he allowed her hands to fall back to her lap. "Your father gave you real pearls that night of your birthday," he said. "I thought it was a fitting gift. Pearls for a pearl. Roy always knew what was right for you."

He turned his gaze back out to the auction ring. Andrea watched him light a cigarette and wondered if he was trying to remind her of the differences between them. Even so, Andrea could have told him that Roy hadn't always known what was right for her or he would have known Tony was the only man for her.

But there was no use in telling him that, Andrea decided. He didn't want to hear that she loved him.

Tony suddenly rose to his feet and glanced down at her. "I'm going to get us some coffee before the cattle start selling. Want something else?"

Her eyes tinged with sadness, she looked up at him and shook her head. "No. Nothing else."

The afternoon had grown late and hot by the time Andrea and Tony returned to the ranch. Tony went straight down to the barns to join the men. Andrea changed into a cooler blouse and went to the kitchen to find Rosita.

"I was beginning to wonder what happened to you two," Rosita said as Andrea pushed through the swinging doors. "The sale must have been a big one. I expected you home earlier."

"It was a big one," Andrea agreed. "Have any ice tea?"

The housekeeper pointed toward the refrigerator. "A whole pitcher."

Andrea fetched a glass from the cabinets and quickly filled it with tea and ice.

"Well, how did it go?" Rosita asked as she put two tins filled with dough into the oven.

Andrea took a sip of the tea, then smiled faintly as Rosita straightened up and planted her hands on her hips.

"Good, I think. The cattle weighed out very well and Tony seemed to be very pleased about the whole thing."

The woman smiled broadly. "That's good, *niña*. Maybe you won't have to sell any more cattle."

Andrea shook her head. "I hope not. I need every cow and heifer I can hold on to now."

Rosita nodded with grim understanding and Andrea swallowed the last of her drink.

"I'm going to the study to do some bookkeeping. Will supper be ready very soon?"

"An hour. I'll call you," she told Andrea. "Where's Tony?"

"At the stable, I think. He wanted to go over a few things with Windell. Now that Larry is gone, he thinks Windell should step in as foreman."

Rosita's black brows lifted thoughtfully. "Windell's pretty young."

"Tony says that he was, too, when he took over as foreman. He thinks Windell has a lot of initiative and potential. And I trust Tony's judgment. If I didn't, I wouldn't have asked for his help in the first place."

The older woman snorted. "But Tony had someone here to guide him along. Lord help us, who does he think is going to be guiding Windell? The other men? They have to be told when to get in the shade and when to get out of it."

In spite of all the problems, Andrea laughed and started toward the door. "It'll be all right, Rosita. Sara will be in school this fall and then I can spend more time out with the men."

"I can't imagine Tony liking that idea."

The smile fell away from Andrea's face. "Tony won't be here, so it could hardly matter to him."

Andrea pushed on through the doors and headed to the study. In the kitchen Rosita shook her head sadly and went back to her cooking.

The sun had long ago slid behind the distant mountains when Andrea left the house and purposefully headed down to the stables.

Rosita had served dinner some time ago, but Tony had not made an appearance. Since they'd returned from the stockyards earlier today Andrea had not seen him once. She felt he was intentionally avoiding her, and that idea hurt very much.

"Hey, Tony! That hackamore really did the trick. Look how calm and straight she's holding her head!"

As Andrea neared the wooden corral, she caught the sound of Windell's voice. When she reached the railing, she could see he was riding Moonbeam, the filly Andrea had raised from a baby. Since they'd broken her to ride, the young mare had continually shaken her head nervously, sometimes even reared up on her hind legs. At the moment, she was behaving perfectly and Tony was grinning with satisfaction as he stood in the middle of the dusty corral watching Windell urge Moonbeam into a smooth short lope.

"She felt boxed in with the tie down and bits," Tony told him. "She just wanted some freedom."

"Now, why didn't I think of that?" Andrea said suddenly.

Unaware that Andrea had been anywhere near, Tony was surprised at the sound of her voice. He turned and saw that she had climbed up on the bottom rail of the corral and was leaning out over the top one.

The special smile she always saved for him was on her face. Reluctantly he walked over to her. As he drew closer he wondered, as he had so many times this past week, why she had to be so beautiful, so endearing, so much a part of him.

"Hello," she said.

"Hello," he replied to her warm sexy voice.

"I thought I might find you down here. Why didn't you come to the house for supper?"

The south desert wind licked at her dark hair. Tony watched her shake it back from her face with a totally unconscious, provocative movement.

"I wasn't hungry," he answered.

His gaze went back to Windell and the filly. Andrea said, "Moonbeam seems very contented now. You've thoroughly astounded Windell. He's been working with her for weeks. You come along and straighten her out in a matter of minutes."

"Does that surprise you?"

Her eyes glinted merrily. "You know it doesn't. You could always do anything you wanted with a horse."

Tony's mouth quirked with the hint of a modest grin. "I just whispered something in her ear."

Andrea chuckled. "I'll just bet you did, Tony Ramirez."

She jumped down from the corral fence and stood next to him. Windell noticed her arrival and waved happily.

"Hey, you're gonna love her now!" he called to Andrea. "Can you believe this?"

Andrea smiled and waved back at him. "That's great, Windell! Keep up the good work."

Both she and Tony watched the young mare for a few more moments, yet Andrea had the feeling that neither of them was thinking of the horse.

After a while, she lifted her gaze to his face. "I'm going riding. Will you come with me?"

Tony studied her with a quiet, steady intensity. Andrea held her breath, praying with everything inside her that he wouldn't refuse. He was going home tomorrow. She needed this last chance to be with him, this last chance to make him see how much he meant to her.

"Yes. I'll come with you."

Such simple words, yet they were a struggle for Tony to say. Still, he had said them because he knew that for him to go riding with her would make her happy. And whatever doubts he might be feeling, there was a part of Tony that wanted to please Andrea, to make her happy.

Silently they walked together to the stables. Andrea helped him gather the tack, then brush and saddle the horses. Soon they were riding across the open fields; Andrea on Odds Maker and Tony on the dun.

The Rio Grande was not far away. In silent agreement, they turned their mounts in the direction of the river. With the dusk had come a balmy breeze. Andrea rolled up the sleeves of her shirt and luxuriated in the feel of it on her face and in her hair.

"As soon as I get the check on the cattle, I'll go to the bank and take care of the first note," she told him after they'd traveled a few minutes.

"I know it won't be pleasant to see all that money go for nothing," he said. "I knew Roy liked to deal big. I suppose that's how he built this ranch in the first place. I just didn't know he was that much of a gambler."

Andrea shrugged. "It's a waste to fret over it now. And in a way, I'll be glad to get it all over with. Once the mortgages are paid off I can put Dad's mistakes behind me. I'll be starting over, but I'll be starting over on my own. If mistakes are made now, at least they'll be my own."

The two horses were abreast of each other. At times their stirrups rubbed together. Tony barely had to turn his head to see Andrea's face. Her expression was tinged with sadness, and the sight of it tore at the tender part of him. "I know the ranch seems bare now with that many head of cattle gone," he said quietly.

She nodded. "Yes, it does." But it will seem even more barren if you go, Tony, she thought.

"Papa always told us boys to never gripe about our bills, just be glad we have the money to pay them."

Andrea's smile was whimsical. "Luis is a wise man, but I guess I don't have to tell you that. Your parents are the only family I have now. I don't know what I'd do without them."

His eyes softened on her face. "After having six sons, my parents wanted a daughter more than anything. Now they have two. You and Sara."

Andrea shifted restlessly in the saddle. In the quietness, the sound of the creaking leather seemed magnified. So did the beating of her heart.

"Tony, what will you do when you go back to Albuquerque?"

"What do you mean?"

"I mean, how will you spend your time? How do you live from day to day?"

He nudged back the brim of his hat and rubbed his fingers across his forehead. "You should know how much work is involved in ranching, Andrea. It keeps me very busy, but if I have some spare time, I use it to work with the mustangs."

"But don't you get lonely? Don't you see friends—a woman?"

He cut her a rueful look. "A woman? What makes you ask that?"

She felt her cheeks growing warm and her heart thudding painfully in her breast. "I—just thought maybe there was someone up there waiting for you to come home. After—after last night I—"

"Andrea," he began, "last night would be better forgotten."

His expression was suddenly aloof, but Andrea wasn't going to allow him to put her off. "Do you have a woman up there, Tony? One that means more to you than—than me?"

One lean finger came up and tugged the hat back down on his forehead. When he turned to look at her, his eyes were hidden by its brim and its shadow. Andrea would have given much to see what was in those hazel eyes at this moment.

Tony looked at her and thought that he should lie and say yes, there was a woman. But he couldn't deceive Andrea. It would be like lying to himself.

"No," he said a little roughly. "There isn't a woman."

Chapter Ten

Relief poured through Andrea like a warm summer rain. Tony might not care enough to stay, but at least he cared for her more than anyone else.

Impulsively she tapped Odds Maker with the heels of her boots and bolted past him. "Beat you to the river!" she taunted over her shoulder.

Taking up her challenge, Tony urged the dun into a gallop. Andrea had not exaggerated when she'd told him the horse could run. He expected the dun to overtake them easily, yet Andrea reached the riverbank a good two lengths before him.

Laughing joyously over the victory, Andrea slid from the saddle and patted the sorrel's sweaty neck.

Tony was irritated with her for running the horses when near darkness shadowed the ground. Still, he smiled to see her so happy about beating him.

"Maybe we should take him back to the track," he suggested wryly.

She laughed, while behind her Odds Maker blew heavily through dilated nostrils. "Do you think we could make more money with him than with the cattle?" she asked.

"No," he said dryly. "But at least I wouldn't be losing any more races."

She clucked her tongue at him, pleased to see he could still joke with her.

The dun's sides heaved beneath him and the saddle. Tony climbed down and began to lead the horse in a quiet walk. Andrea fell in close beside him.

For long moments they walked along in silence, letting the horses cool and catch their wind. It had grown completely dark, making it hard to see the sluggish current of the river just to the left of them, but all the same, they were both aware of the border.

It reminded Andrea of last night and how Tony had talked about a border being between the two of them. The thought was a sobering one.

She looked up at the strong line of his face etched by the starlight and her heart contracted painfully. "Will you be happy, Tony, back on the Rocking R?"

Her voice wobbled on the last words. The sound tore at Tony's heart. Everything inside him wanted to turn and pull her into his arms, comfort her and assure her he would never leave. "Does that really matter?" he asked huskily.

"You know that it does."

He said nothing and the silence was maddening to Andrea. She remembered that Tony had always had the habit of not talking just at the time she wanted him to talk the most.

"I'd like to think that you'll be happy," she ventured on. "But I want you to know that I won't be."

Tony's steps halted as he looked down at her. "Why?"

They were standing very close together. When she looked up, his face was so near and so beautiful. She took a moment to let her eyes drink their fill of his features. In the past she had thought of him so often, had ached to see the mocking little half grin he used to give her, the bedeviled glint in his eyes. How could this one week with him possibly be enough to live the rest of her life on?

"Because you won't be here with me," she answered in a husky voice. Her hands reached out; her fingers curled into his denim shirt. "I won't get to see your face, your smile. I won't get to touch you, to—to kiss you."

By the time she spoke the last words, she'd gone up on her tiptoe and her mouth was just a fraction of an inch away from his.

"Andrea," he whispered. "This can't be."

The warmth of his body pulled at her. She leaned into him until the front of her was pressed against him. "It can be, Tony. If only you'll let it."

His eyelids dropped as he focused on the soft sweetness of her mouth. Andrea watched the desire move across his face and felt her own body melt against him.

"We could both be hurt. You don't need that, Andrea. You've already had enough problems in your life."

Her head gave one shake from side to side as she closed the fraction of space between their lips. "I'm not afraid of you hurting me. You'd never hurt me, Tony. Not if you loved me."

A moan escaped him as he leaned down to kiss her. Her lips tasted just as sweet and precious as they had the night before, and Tony marveled at the fact that she wanted him. Andrea could have any man, but she wanted him. The idea made him drunk with excitement. She made him drunk with excitement!

With a ragged breath he tore his lips away from hers. "You don't know what you're saying, Andrea. We haven't seen each other in a long time. I was a friend and now I've helped you. You're getting gratitude confused with love."

Her eyes lifted slowly to his and Tony's stomach clenched at the smoky desire he saw hidden between her lashes.

"No, Tony," she said. "Seeing you again has shown me that I never knew what love really was until now. I was too young to recognize it when you left six years ago. If I had, things might have turned out far differently. That's why I can't let you go. Not when I know it could be so good for us."

"Good for us," he repeated in a mocking voice. "How could it be good for you, Andrea? What do I have to offer you? Even with the problems you're having right now, you could sell the Rio Vista and buy me out twice over."

She looked at him with utter frustration. "Do you think that's all I care about? Money? Luxuries? I thought you knew me better than that, Tony."

He raised his hand and cupped her face. She knew as she looked into his eyes that this fierce love for him would never stop, never fade.

"When a man takes a woman, Andrea, he wants to be able to give her all the things she can't give herself. He wants her to be able to look up to him and know that he's her protector, her provider. Maybe you would just call that machismo, Andrea. But it's what I am inside."

"I understand that you have your pride, Tony," she said gently. "But there is something you don't understand. There's only one thing a woman really wants or needs from a man and that's his love. True love from his heart. But I guess that's asking for more than you can give," she said with sad finality.

He said nothing to deny her words and that silence in itself wounded her. Slowly she turned away from him and reached blindly for the stirrup on Odds Maker's saddle.

He was there to stop her before she had the chance to swing up onto the horse's back. His hands clenched her shoulders desperately. "Damn it, Andrea!" he grated, spinning her around to face him. "What are you trying to do to me? To you? We were friends. Why ruin it by trying to make it into more?"

The feel of his hands drove everything from her mind. At that moment there were only two things consuming her thoughts: love and desire. She swayed toward him, the heat of his body drawing her like a magnet.

"I don't want to be just your friend, Tony," she whispered desperately. "I want to be your lover, too."

Andrea heard the guttural sound of surrender in the back of his throat as his hands crushed her up against him. She wound her arms around his neck and tugged his head down.

He kissed her blindly, hungrily, and Andrea wilted with the need to give herself to him. It seemed he'd always been a part of her heart. She wanted him to be a part of her body, too. She wanted their hearts and minds and bodies to meet and become one, not just for tonight, but forever.

"Tony, my darling," she murmured breathlessly. "I love you. You have to know that."

His mouth had forsaken hers to slide with sweet torment against her throat. "I know," he said, his husky voice muffled by her skin, "that for years you have bewitched me. Your face, your smile. Your words. Your body." His head lifted and his thumb and forefinger curled around her chin. With the slightest pressure, he tilted her face up toward him and the inky sky above their heads. "Just looking at you is a sweet seduction."

The intensity of his green-brown eyes seared her with heat. The smoky drawl of his voice pierced everything feminine inside her. Hot urgency swept through her, washing her with a mindless need. Her fingers traveled to the center of his chest and fumbled with the snap on his shirt. When it came undone, she quickly progressed downward until the last snap was freed. With slow deliberate movements she pulled the tails of his shirt from the waistband of his jeans, then sighed with pleasure as her palms flattened against his warm satiny skin.

Whether his groan was reluctant or filled with need, she could not tell. Andrea's senses were incapable of sorting out anything except the hot ravage of his mouth on hers, the desperate dance of their tongues, the desire between them that was mounting even higher.

"Andrea—my Lord—this is—"

"Good. Right," she finished his half-choked protest.

She pressed light kisses across his chest until she reached a flat nipple. Slowly, tormentingly, her tongue outlined it. Andrea felt his fingers tighten against the curve of her bottom, drawing her even closer.

Andrea's knees became liquid at the intimate contact. Just when she thought they would buckle, Tony gently lowered her and himself to the ground.

Stubby grass and small rocks jabbed at her back, but Andrea hardly noticed. She only knew his warm body was sparking magic inside her, filling her with a wondrous ache that was something akin to pain. He carried the earthy scent of man and the sweet scent of himself. She drank in her fill of the fragrance, letting her lips savor the salty tang of his skin.

Tony fumbled with the buttons on her shirt, then pushed aside the flimsy white lace covering her breasts. The hot blinding need to have her blocked right and wrong from his mind. He could only think how much he craved and needed her. No other woman could do this to him and the reason was very simple. Love. It was the bridge that connected the physical and the spiritual. The blend was powerful, heady and everything that Tony had ever yearned for.

Andrea was moaning, whispering his name as Tony planted rough moist kisses across her breasts and struggled to pull the tight jeans down over her hips.

She reached to help him. At the same moment a horse nickered somewhere in the distance.

Neither Andrea nor Tony registered the sound until the shrill answering whinny from Odds Maker shattered the silence.

"What the hell—" Tony muttered as Odds Maker neighed again.

Andrea lifted herself up on one arm just in time to see the horse wheel and take off in a dead run back toward the ranch.

The sudden interruption sobered Tony. He glanced down at Andrea. Her face looked as dazed as he felt. It was incredible how lost in her he'd been!

Still addled with desire, Tony wiped a hand across his face, then forced himself to roll away from her.

Andrea sat up, peered at the shadows around them, then over at Tony. They'd been so close to making love. But now the moment was over and all she could do was wonder whether it would have changed things.

"The horses took off?" she asked, her voice still husky.

The arm across Tony's eyes fell away. Andrea watched him rise slowly to his feet and jam his shirt-tails back inside his jeans. Her body ached for him, but obviously he'd put aside any need he might have had for her.

"One of them. Yours. The dun is right over there."

"Damn horse!" she muttered angrily. Why had he chosen just that moment to stage his getaway? Sighing, she rose to her feet and refastened her clothes.

"At least he kept us from making a big mistake," Tony told her.

Andrea slapped the dust from her jeans with angry swats. "Mistake? Tony, that doesn't even warrant a response."

"Then don't give me one," he said resignedly. "I don't want to hear any more about it."

She watched him stride into the shadows to retrieve the dun, who was grazing leisurely some few feet away.

"I guess now you're going to tell me that you didn't want to make love to me," she said sadly.

He loomed back out of the night shadows, the horse closely following his heels. There were only inches separating them when he halted in front of her.

"Whatever my faults have been, Andrea, I've never lied to you."

His voice was unexpectedly soft and gentle. It shattered the frustration inside her. She reached out and lightly touched his arm.

"If I had made love to you, there would be no turning back for me. I'd have to stay," he went on.

"And what would be so wrong with that?" she asked.

He shook his head. "All my life, Andrea, I've had to cross borders and barriers to get where I am. I've been lucky so far, but I've watched some of my friends struggle to get across, to build a life for themselves. They're so busy looking back over their shoulders in fear that they can't move forward. Loving you would be crossing another border for me, Andrea. Living with you would have me looking back, reminding me what you've always had and what I will never have. I'd wind up doubting myself and blaming you." He pulled away from her and reached for the stirrup on the dun's saddle. "Neither one of us needs that. The best thing I can do for both of us now is to go."

Pain and frustration swamped Andrea as she watched him swing into the dun's saddle. He was so wrong. She had to make him see it!

Opening her mouth, she started to protest, but Tony didn't give her the chance.

Stony-faced, he reached down for her hand. Apparently this was all he wanted to say and all he wanted to hear.

Andrea grasped his fingers and stuck her toe in the stirrup. A sudden pull from his hand and she was mounted on the skirt of the saddle just inches behind him.

The dun was skittish from having two riders on his back. After a couple of crow hops that nearly managed to toss her over the horse's hindquarters, Andrea grabbed Tony's waist.

A few minutes passed and the horse finally settled into a slow steady walk. It dawned on Andrea that she could release her hold on Tony. But she didn't. This might be the last time she would get to touch him, and the idea overwhelmed her with sadness.

She wrapped her arms around him and leaned her cheek against his back. In front of her, Tony closed his eyes and covered her hand with his. He'd never been so torn or confused in all his life. Ever since he'd come to El Paso with her, he'd done nothing but contradict himself. It was because what he needed and what he wanted were two different things, he realized.

He loved Andrea; loved her more than he'd ever expected to love anyone. But hadn't he heard somewhere that really loving someone meant letting them go?

The afternoon was growing late, but Andrea wasn't aware of it. Since Tony had left this morning, she'd done little more than sit out on the balcony of her bedroom and stare across the desert range.

Tony's departure had left her physically numb. Her mind seemed to be the only thing working at the moment, and it was doing overtime.

Sighing wearily, she rubbed her aching eyes and allowed her head to drop back against the lawn chair.

The ranch lay below her in all its glory, still one of the biggest spreads around El Paso, and still safely hers. Tony had helped her pull things together. She had a marginal herd of good cows and calves left. It was enough to build on.

Andrea should have been happy about the whole thing, but she'd never been more miserable in her life. None of it had any meaning now that Tony was gone.

Listlessly she rose to her feet and leaned over the balustrade. The air was hot, the shadows growing longer. Andrea knew she needed to pull herself together, go downstairs and join the others. But her heart just wasn't in it. She didn't want to see Rosita's sad face or answer Sara's persistent questions about Tony.

When is he coming back, Mama? How soon can we go to Albuquerque to see him? When I wake up tomorrow, will Tony be back then? Andrea groaned as Sara's little voice replayed in her thoughts.

Sara had cried with a broken heart this morning when Tony had driven away. But now the child had dried her tears and put on a brave face because Andrea had told her that Tony wouldn't want her to cry and that they would see him soon.

Andrea knew that none of them would see him soon. But she couldn't let Sara know that now. It would be easier on the child for time to tell her.

It wasn't right, Andrea thought with a bit of anger. She loved Tony. It didn't matter what she owned or what he owned or what circumstances either one of them had been born into.

So he wasn't wealthy monetarily, she said to herself. But in all things that mattered he was rich. He was a good honorable man, a man who'd set standards for himself and worked hard to achieve them. How could he not think he would be enough for her?

If she'd only had more time, she thought. If he hadn't left, Andrea might have eventually made him see it. That was probably the reason he'd gone, to make sure Andrea wouldn't have the chance to change his mind. He was running like a coward from a woman who loved him. She felt like driving up there and telling him so!

Andrea suddenly bolted to her feet. *Why not?* Why not drive up there and tell him? He could only run so far. And if she was woman enough to oversee this ranch and raise a daughter single-handedly, she was woman enough to go after the man she loved.

Tony might live on his pride, but Andrea was willing to sacrifice some of hers. Tony was worth it, and she was going to make him see that!

In five minutes' time she'd thrown a few things into an overnight bag and changed into a lilac cotton jumpsuit.

She plaited her hair into one long braid, quickly dabbed on some makeup, then hurried out of the room.

"Sara! Rosita!" she called when she was halfway down the staircase.

"In here, Mama."

Sara's voice came from the study. Andrea found her daughter with a polishing rag and a can of furniture oil. Rosita was about to plug in the vacuum cleaner.

The old woman looked up when Andrea entered the room carrying her overnight bag in one hand and her purse in the other.

Planting her hands on either side of her broad hips, Rosita asked in a surprised tone, "Are you going somewhere?"

"Are you, Mama? *Are* you?" Sara parroted while tugging on Andrea's arm.

Andrea looked down at her daughter and nodded, then back up at Rosita. "I'm going to Albuquerque to see Tony."

Rosita said nothing. She merely looked at Andrea for a long time then walked across to her and kissed both her cheeks.

"Be careful, *niña*," she said with stern affection.

"Then you don't think I'm doing the wrong thing?"

Rosita shook her head back and forth. "It's never wrong to follow your heart."

Andrea blinked at the moisture stinging her eyes, then knelt down to pull Sara into her embrace. "I want you to be a good girl for Rosita and I'll be back as soon as I can."

"Are you going to make Tony come home, Mama?"

Andrea smiled faintly and brushed the wisp of stray hairs away from her daughter's eyes. "I can't make him come home, darling. But I'm going to ask him to."

More than two hours later, Andrea passed through the outskirts of Truth or Consequences. A glance at her watch said a quarter of eight; however, it looked much later. The sky was almost dark now.

Andrea took a good look out the car window and discovered why. Purple and gray clouds were gathering in the north and west. What little sunlight remained was being blotted out by the squall line.

Ten miles passed when the first rain began to splatter the windshield. Streaks of lightning bolted over the mountaintops with increasing frequency.

Andrea knew she was in for a desert rainstorm. At this time of year, they formed in the late evening, sometimes dumping rain for only a few minutes and sometimes for a couple of hours or more.

Normally, she loved the rain. But she knew the wet slick highway would force her to slow down for safety's sake. She hoped she would drive out of the storm—at least by the time she reached Socorro.

A weather report might give her a clue to what she was heading into. Andrea reached for the radio knob when a sudden loud pop caused her to jerk with fright.

Her first thought was that lightning had struck close to the car and merely frightened her. But the sudden wrench of the steering wheel told her it was much more. Her back tire had blown.

A few feet ahead she spotted a wide level spot on the side of the highway. Andrea allowed the car to crawl slowly toward it while each flop of the tire made her want to groan with frustration.

Andrea turned off the motor, leaned back against the seat and let out a deep sigh. How was she going to work this? she wondered. The rain was still just a sprinkle, but there was a dandy electrical storm raging outside the car.

Just the thought of being out in this weather made the hair on the backs of her arms prickle. Still, if she sat in the car and waited, there was no guarantee the downpour would slacken. She'd have to get out of the car sometime. She'd be soaked to the skin and still be a target for an electrical bolt before she finished with the tire.

Andrea looked out of the window to her right. In the far distance just this side of the mountains was the Elephant Butte Reservoir. At the moment, streaks of lightning flashed like fireworks over the water. To her left was nothing but the highway and open desert. In this area, even in daylight, there was hardly any traffic. Now, with the dark and the storm, it was practically nonexistent.

She could sit and wait for the storm to end. But that might be two hours or more. She ought to be almost to the Rocking R by then.

Decisively Andrea unsnapped her seat belt and reached for the door handle. She hadn't traveled all this distance to be struck by lightning or stranded for two hours. She'd grit her teeth, change the tire as quickly as she could and be on her way.

The air had grown much cooler now. Andrea shivered as she raised the trunk to retrieve the jack. Rain pelted her head and shoulders as she worked. She knew this was nothing, however, compared to what the rain would become in just a matter of minutes.

She'd exchanged the flat tire for the good spare and was tightening the last lug nut when she heard the sound of an approaching vehicle. Andrea didn't take the time to stand up and look. She was wet, her clothes and hands smeared with dirt and grease, but she was almost finished. It was too late to look for help.

"Andrea! What in God's name are you doing out here?"

Andrea nearly dropped the tire iron at the sound of Tony's voice. Her head jerked around to see him standing over her, a look of astonishment on his face.

Stunned, she rose slowly to her feet. For a few seconds all she could do was look at him as the lightning streaked above them and the rain grew heavier and heavier. He was like a beautiful part of the desert come out of nowhere, straight to her.

"I—I—was going to see you," she said finally. "What are you doing out here?"

Tony looked at her and Andrea suddenly knew everything was going to be all right. There was love on his face. Love for her.

"I was coming back to you," he said.

He'd come back to her all on his own! Andrea's groan of joy was drowned out by a loud clap of thunder. She took one step toward him and Tony made up the rest of the distance.

They reached for each other with their arms and their lips. For long moments they kissed hungrily and ignored the rain and the lightning coming down around them.

Andrea thought how hard and warm and so very beloved he felt to her. This man stirred her body and her heart. She would never get enough of him, never stop loving him.

It was Tony who finally ended the embrace and pushed her into the cab of his pickup and out of the rain.

Water dripped off the brim of his hat and splashed on her face as he hauled her close against him.

Laughing, Andrea wiped it away and looked into his eyes. The love she saw there stole her breath away.

"I couldn't believe it when I saw you and the car," he murmured. "Why were you coming to see me tonight, out in this storm?"

She smiled at him and lifted her hand to touch his face. "I wasn't going to let night or a storm or a flat tire stop me," she said with conviction. "I was determined to see you and tell you that you were making a mistake. Why were you coming back?''

His white smile flashed in his dark face. ''To tell you I love you,'' he said simply. ''That I don't want to live without you.''

''Then you're going to marry me?''

The smile on his face deepened. ''You know what everyone will say, don't you? They'll say I'm marrying you for your money and that you're marrying me for my looks.''

Andrea suddenly burst out with happy laughter. ''Oh Lord, Tony, I thought you were going to say so that I'd have you to run the ranch for me.''

Tony's hand slid behind the back of her head and drew her mouth up to his.

''We'll run the ranch together,'' he said huskily after he'd kissed her. ''We'll do everything together.''

''All week you've been telling me that we shouldn't be together, that the difference between us was too great. What made you change your mind?'' she asked.

Andrea felt his shoulder lift and fall against her. ''When I got back to the Rocking R, it all looked so empty and lonely. I kept seeing your face and I kept remembering what you said—about love being the thing a woman really wanted the most,'' he said. ''And I thought, damn Tony, you've done all this yourself. You've climbed up from nothing to own a good ranch, and you didn't do it by being afraid to try. Andrea loves you, you love Andrea.'' His mouth quirked with a soft little smile as his fingers lifted and smoothed over her cheek. ''And you know what? I'm just cocky and conceited enough to think I have everything you'll ever need.''

A happy sigh rushed from deep inside her as she tightened her hold on him. "You do, Tony," she whispered fervently. "And it's all right in here." She rubbed her hand across his heart and smiled up into his eyes. "Just don't ever stop loving me. Don't ever leave again."

His face was suddenly serious. "I didn't recognize the way you felt about me all those years ago, Andrea. Maybe it would have changed things, I don't know. I just know that at the time I believed I was doing the right thing. You were very young and I had nothing to offer any woman, much less you. I had a need inside me to start out on my own, to prove myself as a man. Your father asked me to leave because he thought I wasn't good enough. That does something to a man's pride, Andrea. I was determined to prove him wrong."

"You proved him wrong, Tony, when you came back just now," Andrea murmured, her lips tilting with a soft smile.

An arrogant glint suddenly came in his eyes and she felt his fingers begin to loosen the buttons between her breasts. "You'd have hell running me off now, woman."

"Love me, Tony," she said.

"I will."

Epilogue

The moon hung over the Rio Grande. Its yellow beams painted the ranch with rich color and filtered through the glass doors, spreading a glow over the bed and the two lovers.

Andrea stretched with languid contentment and slid away from her husband's warm body.

"Where are you going, *chica*?"

At Tony's low question, Andrea glanced back over her bare shoulder. A soft smile tilted the corners of her lips. "Missing me already?"

"Yes. Come back to bed." His voice was still husky from making love with her only minutes ago. Still, his lean brown hand slid invitingly across the empty space beside him.

Andrea chuckled as she pulled on her robe and crossed to the dressing table to pick up her hairbrush. "Have you forgotten that we're going to the livestock auction this morning?"

He rolled onto his back and watched her movements through lazily slitted eyes. The eagerness in her voice would have made one think Tony was taking her to the Bahamas instead of a dusty sale barn, and the thought made his lips curve with amusement.

Over the past year, Tony had learned that Andrea was not predictable, spoiled or afraid of work. He'd learned that her love for him had been just as true and deep as she'd told him in the beginning. And he'd also learned that when two people lived as one and loved as one, that all the bridges, gaps and borders disappeared.

"Andrea," he drawled, "it's still dark outside. The moon is out, the stars are shining."

Andrea turned to look out the sliding glass doors. "How romantic of you to notice, Tony," she said coyly, pulling the brush through her tousled hair.

"No one will even be up for another hour," he continued in a low suggestive voice.

Andrea laughed softly, walked back to the bedside and looked down at him. "That's true," she agreed. "And there's also that matter of Sara telling everyone her mother and daddy are going to give her a baby brother. You haven't forgotten that, have you?"

His chuckle was sexy and loving. "I'm willing to work very hard on that matter this morning, Andrea. Again."

"You lusty Latin," she murmured pleasurably.

The next moment her robe fell back to the floor and Tony was reaching for her. By the time they went downstairs to breakfast, the sun had chased the moon and stars from the sky, but not from Tony and Andrea's eyes.

* * *

Later at the auction, Tony sat back and watched
with an indulgent little smile as his wife bid on twenty
head of steers. They were good-looking cattle, going
for a good price. She was doing a fine job of bidding,
and it looked as if the man across the way was going
to back down and let her have them.

To say Tony was proud of Andrea would be an un-
derstatement. Yet he was kind of proud of himself,
too. He'd taught her everything she knew about cattle
buying. But today Tony wasn't going to remind her of
that. He wanted her to think she'd done it all on her
own. And this time she had.

"Sold to Mrs. Tony Ramirez!"

Tony leaned forward from his relaxed position.
"Damn, Andrea, you've been down here so much they
know you by name," he said close to her ear.

She shot him a pleased smile. "That's because both
our ranches are doing so well that we can buy and sell
a lot more these days."

After they'd married, Andrea had insisted that Tony
not sacrifice his ranch in Albuquerque just because
he'd married her. He'd worked hard for the ranch. It
wasn't just a place or a piece of land. It represented a
big accomplishment in his life. That made it just as
important to Andrea as it was to Tony.

Together, they'd decided to keep both ranches and
alternate their time between the two. While they were
away from the Rio Vista, Windell was doing a good
job of keeping things running smoothly. On the other
hand, when the two of them were back in El Paso,
Zelda's husband looked after things on the Rocking R.
Combining the capital of both ranches had helped to
strengthen both of them.

"Well, Tony, they know you by name, too," Andrea went on. "How could they not?" She smiled and mused aloud, "Come to think of it, they probably believe we're connected at the hip or something and can't be separated."

Beneath his hat brim, Tony's eyes squinted sexily back at her. "They might even think we're in love."

A slow smile spread across her face. She reached over, put her arm around him and whispered in his ear. "You know, Tony, they could just be right."

*   *   *   *   *

COMING NEXT MONTH

#622 A MAN CALLED TRAVERS—Brittany Young
City sophisticate Eden Sloane never dreamed she'd love the great
outdoors...until she met rugged Australian cattle rancher
Jack Travers.

#623 COURTNEY'S CONSPIRACY—Christine Flynn
Vivacious Courtney Fairchild and reserved Steven Powers had
conspired to make a match between their lonely relatives. But
then they discovered that their *own* match might be made
in heaven....

#624 LORD OF THE GLEN—Frances Lloyd
Nicola Sharman wanted the scoop on the mysterious lord of a
Scottish manor, but Angus McPherson, his dashing gamekeeper,
gave her heart a story worth writing home about!

#625 HEART OF THE MATTER—Linda Varner
Pediatrician Prescott Holter was looking for the perfect wife, and
Dallas Delaney was too fun-loving for such a serious job. So why
couldn't he stop thinking about her?

#626 WILD HORSE CANYON—Elizabeth August
They married out of obligation, and their families had feuded for
generations, but could feisty Maggie Randolph and irresistible
Joe Colbert forge a bond of love for the generations to come?

#627 THE PASSIONS OF KATE MADIGAN—Suzanne Forster
On the outside, police academy drill instructor Kate Madigan was
tough, but her new recruit—dark, intriguing Ty Raphaell—knew
he could reach her hidden passion....

AVAILABLE THIS MONTH:

ATTRACTIVE, SPACE SAVING BOOK RACK

Display your most prized novels on this handsome and sturdy book rack. The hand-rubbed walnut finish will blend into your library decor with quiet elegance, providing a practical organizer for your favorite hard-or soft-covered books.

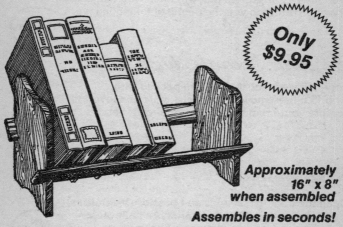

Only $9.95

Approximately 16" x 8" when assembled

Assembles in seconds!

To order, rush your name, address and zip code, along with a check or money order for $10.70* ($9.95 plus 75¢ postage and handling) payable to *Silhouette Books*.

Silhouette Books
Book Rack Offer
901 Fuhrmann Blvd.
P.O. Box 1396
Buffalo, NY 14269-1396

Offer not available in Canada.

*New York and Iowa residents add appropriate sales tax.

BKR-2A

FOUR UNIQUE SERIES
FOR EVERY WOMAN YOU ARE . . .

Silhouette Romance

Love, at its most tender, provocative, emotional . . . in stories that will make you laugh and cry while bringing you the magic of falling in love.

6 titles per month

Silhouette Special Edition

Sophisticated, substantial and packed with emotion, these powerful novels of life and love will capture your imagination and steal your heart.

6 titles per month

Silhouette Desire

Open the door to romance and passion. Humorous, emotional, compelling—yet always a believable and sensuous story—Silhouette Desire never fails to deliver on the promise of love.

6 titles per month

Silhouette Intimate Moments

Enter a world of excitement, of romance heightened by suspense, adventure and the passions every woman dreams of. Let us sweep you away.

4 titles per month